BODY ON THE SHORE

Gripping crime fiction set in Liverpool

DIANE M. DICKSON

D1213556

Published by The Book Folks

London, 2020

ISBN 978-1-913516-82-6

www.thebookfolks.com

For Richard.

Prologue

Beatrice had always been afraid of the dark. Not so scared that it was a problem. Just a small quickening of her heartbeat, a tiny tingle of dread somewhere down in the pit of her stomach. Of course, you shouldn't be afraid of something that doesn't really exist, and the dark is only the lack of light. That's what her mother had always told her. It was the things that might be hidden in the dark that were the cause of her fear. And with what had happened in the last few weeks, everything her mother had told her was now being called into question. Everything.

She knew that the chances of something really being there were very slim. At least, that was what she had made herself believe.

The noise in the night was small and indistinct. A cat, she thought, hunting in the alley. A dog possibly. But nothing to worry about, nothing to fear. Ironically, it was as she turned on the light that the danger came.

She fought hard, gave it everything she could. She clawed at his face and dragged at the bag and drew in panicked breaths. She mustn't let it cover her mouth. She was dizzied and terrified, but she fought on until, at the end, apart from the pain, intense and stultifying, there was also a vague sort of indignant surprise. It seemed that she had been right about the dark all along.

Chapter 1

DI Jordan Carr took off his jacket and hung it over the back of his chair. He removed the lid from his takeaway cup so that he could enjoy the aroma of his Americano.

While he waited for the computer to boot, he fished into the bag of pastries. He'd already eaten that morning with Harry and Penny but had treated himself to a croissant and a chocolatine. Maybe when he hit his forties, he'd need to be more careful, but that was a few years off yet. He worked out regularly and went running three times a week, so the extra calories didn't appear to be doing him any harm right now. He was tall enough to carry a couple of extra kilos, he reckoned, but if he started to get too chunky Nana Gloria and some of his more 'honest' cousins would be quick to let him know. Nana Gloria had a bit of a thing for Idris Elba and kept on about facial hair: "Just a little bit, Jordan. Stubble, that's what they call it. You'd look just like him and he's a policeman as well."

There was no point telling her he was an actor, Nana Gloria believed what she wanted to. Anyway, it wasn't happening. When he'd let it grow there were a few grey hairs in among the black, which depressed him. Anyway, Penny was one hundred per cent against it.

Mornings would soon be different, when Penny started back at work and Harry went to the nursery. He was sorry about that. He relished the family time and it warmed him to know they were safe at home in Crosby while he was at work.

But Penny was ready to get back to work. She had come so far since the days in Oxford, just after Josh arrived, when she had been lost in the fug of depression. They had come through it and, though she loved spending time with their son, she needed something more.

The computer was booted. He wiped the grease from his fingers, tossed the empty cup and the papers into the bin and leaned forward to scroll through the overnight messages. There wasn't that much. A couple of fights in the city centre, the usual crop of car thefts and some attempted break-ins. He could spend the morning catching up on paperwork.

Then his internal phone rang.

* * *

DCI Cross stood looking out of his window. The glass was grubby and wet and the scene outside, dull and grey. The view was of the tiny bit of green in front of the station, the litter-strewn road and the low-rise flats opposite. It was uninspiring and he pulled the cord to part close the vertical blinds.

"Jordan. Have you got much on at the moment?" he said.

"Nothing too pressing, sir."

"Good. Got an odd one for you. Details have been sent through to you. Young woman found dead this morning, down on the beach. A suspicious death apparently. Medical examiner is over there. CSI should be on scene, the circus is underway. Out near where you live, I reckon. Crosby, isn't it?"

"Yes, sir. So, why have we got it?"

"Don't you want it? Too busy, are you?"

"No, of course not. It's just that there is Waterloo nearer."

"Apparently, they are overstretched right now, some people sick, a few on courses, well you know what it's like. There's no slack in the personnel cover these days. Anyway, they've asked for our help. If you'd prefer me to give it to someone else, I can. I just thought it was about time you took the lead. You've been here a while now, settled in and familiar and all that rot."

"Yes, of course, sir. I'm ready."

"Okay then. Off you go and, DI Carr, try and move this along swiftly. I don't want DCI Campbell from Waterloo on my back every five minutes. Take that new lad with you. DC Denn, isn't it? We might as well throw him in at the deep end. I've heard he's keen."

"A DC, sir."

"Yes. I realise you probably want a detective sergeant, but he's what we've got. Make it work."

"Yes, sir. I'd better get on then."

Jordan managed to keep his tone level and his expression impassive but the DCI was getting under his skin. Impatient, ill-tempered and blasé to the point of rudeness, and if that wasn't enough Richard Cross had raging halitosis.

Jordan grabbed his jacket, rang through to Terry Denn telling him to get down to the car park, signed out, and was in the car within ten minutes of leaving DCI Cross's office. The despatcher had sent the co-ordinates to his smartphone and the Google voice had him heading back along the roads he had travelled just over an hour before.

* * *

The promenade was a pantomime of blue and white. Crime scene tape, cars, uniforms and, of course, growing now, a crowd of onlookers. Officers were trying to move people away, but it was an impossible task. There was a white van with the force logo on the side and boxes of kit

5

near the open rear doors. Jordan took out gloves and shoe covers and moved aside to let the young detective take his own gear. Terry's face was pale and there was a fine sheen of sweat along his upper lip.

"First one?" Jordan asked.

"Yes, sir. I've seen stuff already, traffic and so on. A few nasty smashes, but this is my first suspicious death. It feels different."

"Yes, okay. Most important thing, don't contaminate the scene. Nobody will be impressed if you do that."

Chapter 2

They walked to the head of the slipway.

Out across the wet sand, a small group was gathered around the legs of one of the steel men – sculptures that the artist Antony Gormley had installed. The other ninety-nine statues kept impassive watch from their places in the bay. Jordan approached the bobby with a clipboard and held up his warrant card.

"How do we get down there? Where is the safe route?"

"Isn't one." As he spoke, the man turned. "Best if you don't go down. Not unless you have to."

"I'm SIO on this, I guess I have to."

"Ah right. Well, sir, no way is really safe, not just now. There's the sand, isn't there?"

"The sand?"

"Aye, the sinking sand. All stirred up it is and really unstable. They're going to have to move along. Don't know how they plan on getting the body back. I reckon they'll have to slide it on a bag or something, but whatever, they need to watch themselves. Look now, see."

Jordan peered towards the group as one of the figures called out waving his arms. He twisted back and forth obviously struggling to move his feet and lower legs. Two of the others, outlined against the pale grey of the sky and the darker grey of the water beyond, stepped carefully towards him. To a chorus of jeers and laughter from the onlookers on the shore, he fell backwards with a small splash.

The group around the heap of black plastic had paused in their work to watch. A couple more of them moved forward to help, but by now the little drama was over. As he turned to splash and plod his sodden way towards the promenade, carrying the boots that he had stepped out of, the unfortunate constable raised a hand to acknowledge the jeering from the crowd.

Jordan's glance met that of the embarrassed uniformed officer. They both had thoughts of Morecombe Bay and desperate calls from the cockle pickers. Quicksand, the stuff of nightmares and folk lore, but at times a danger all too real.

"I reckon, you can wait here, Terry. It's not going to be helpful more feet stirring up the surface. Can you deal with things over there?"

He pointed to one of the benches where a woman in an anorak was hunched forward, holding a little dog on her lap. A female officer sat beside her.

"That'll be our witness. Have a word."

Terry watched him for a moment and then stomped away towards the figure on the bench.

Jordan fetched a pair of wellies from the car and dragged on a scene suit over his clothes. The sand near the promenade was dry and powdery but where the tide had touched it the surface was ridged, puddled, and the nearer he came to the statue the more unstable it became. Now and again there was the sharp shock of camera flash against the dull day as pictures were taken. He walked carefully, determined not to give the crowd more entertainment. He was glad he'd brought his boots.

* * *

There would be no point bringing in a crime scene tent. There was nowhere to secure it and the victim would have to be moved before the tide came in. It was an impossible scene to examine in any depth so all they could do was gather what information there was while they had the chance. Jordan crouched beside the medical examiner. She glanced at him and nodded but continued dictating into the little handheld device.

The body was wrapped in two heavy duty refuse sacks, but they had torn where they'd caught on the big steel legs of the statue and then been cut by Phil Grant's knife. Parcel tape had been used to hold the sacks together and remnants still adhered to the plastic.

Dr Grant paused and stood up to ease her back.

"Hiya, Jordan. How come you're here?" she asked.

"Just helping out, Phil."

"Well, if you can wait until we get back up to the car, I'll let you have a full rundown on what I've got so far. No doubt it's suspicious. Suspicious and violent. Poor thing could never have survived the blows to her head, but at least it would have been quick. The end at least."

"How do you mean, the end?"

"Evidence of defence wounds, broken nails and what have you."

She knelt again and pointed with a plastic pen.

Jordan steadied himself with one hand on the uneven surface as he leaned closer to look at the woman. Clots of hair stuck to her face and neck. She was wearing nightclothes, a blue towelling dressing gown and underneath, a pale nightdress with lace around the top. She had been pretty, was still pretty, if you could ignore the gaping wounds on her head.

It was unlikely that the body had been dumped here. She would surely not have been carried across unstable ground, just to be left at that particular point. More likely the corpse had been washed down the River Mersey with the tide and accidently caught on the legs of the statue, otherwise it would have been lost forever in the Irish Sea. Jordan would need to speak to someone about tide tables and currents. This was something new. Since he'd moved to Liverpool from Oxford, he'd come to enjoy the river and the broad flat sands, the ferries, and the container ships, but he hadn't a clue about the ebb and flow of the waters. There wasn't much else to see, and they had limited time. He glanced up at the blank face of the statue and then back to the gory remains.

"I'll see you back at the car," he said.

Phil nodded and continued with her examination.

Terry was sitting with the witness, making notes. He looked up as Jordan joined them. The woman was in her sixties, thin and fit-looking but right now, pale and shaky.

"Detective Inspector this is—"

The woman interrupted him, not wanting anyone stealing the limelight.

"Ewell, Theresa. It's Miss. I was telling your boy here, I come down here every day. Twice, morning and evening. I watch the birds, the boats." She reached beside her and held up a pair of binoculars. "I've done it for years. Me and my da used to come. Habit I suppose, but..." She shrugged. "Why live by the shore and not come to the beach? We used to come before they put up those statues. They are a bit spooky and strange. Big naked men walking out into the estuary like that, but I don't mind them. They're not offensive or anything. They're by that man that did the big Angel aren't they? Gormley – that's his name."

She turned to look over at the small group which was now beginning to move away from the metal giant, dragging the black bags on a plastic stretcher.

"Anyway, Benjie here," she said, stroking the terrier's silky ears, "he ran off and he wouldn't come back. He's not like that. Normally he's a good boy." She leaned forward to plant a quick kiss on the dog's head. "I didn't go down. I usually stick to the top here, on the dry sand.

It's not safe if there's no-one around to go down there. Anyway, he was pulling and dragging at that thing and then when I had a look with the binoculars, I could see it was some poor sod in a bag on the beach. Horrible."

Her eyes filled with tears.

"And you didn't go down there?" Jordan asked.

"No, should I have done? There was no way whoever it is was still alive, not in a plastic bag. I just called you lot."

"No, you did exactly the right thing. I'll have someone take you home if you like. Is there someone who can be with you."

"No, lad, it's fine. I've got my car there and I'm alright. I don't live far away. Just need a nice cuppa and I'll be sorted."

"Have you got all you need, Detective Constable?" Jordan said.

Terry nodded and closed his notebook.

"Okay, I'll send someone later to take a statement, if that's alright. You didn't see anyone, did you? While you were having your walk."

"No, only the usuals, nobody down there at any rate," the woman said.

"Okay, I'll let you go. Thank you so much, Miss Ewell, you've been a great help."

They walked back to where the coroner's van was parked, the rear doors standing open. He lifted his hand to wave at Phil Grant who was now dragging off a sodden, dirt-smeared crime suit.

"Nice to see you again, Jordan. How's your lovely wife?"

"She's well, thanks."

"There's a flask of coffee here. Help yourself."

"Thanks, I will."

She continued to strip off the protective gear and bundled it into a bag.

"So, as you saw, female and young. Probably early twenties. IC1. I'll get to the examination today. Will you come?" she asked.

"Yes, I'll bring Terry as well." As he spoke Jordan was aware of the young detective beside him tensing, he turned. "Your first?"

"Sir."

"Oh well, you have to get it out of the way sometime."

It began to drizzle and there was a chill wind blowing across the estuary. A couple of gulls were arguing about a lump of something nasty lying beside a waste bin. He had no choice but to walk over to make sure it wasn't anything more than just general litter. It was just a discarded sandwich. Jordan left it where it was because someone would have the job of collecting all of the waste, including the disposable nappies and examining them in detail, and he wouldn't risk contaminating anything now he'd taken his gloves off. It was almost certainly a waste of time considering that the body had washed down the Mersey, but a fingertip search would have to be done.

Once she had finished her coffee, Phil dragged off her thick sweater and yanked out the clips that held her long hair. Jordan refilled her mug from the flask, and she reached to take it from him.

"Cheers."

Out of the corner of his eye Jordan was aware of Terry gawping at the medical examiner. Now she was out of the shapeless suit and unglamorous head covering he got his first proper eyeful. Jordan remembered his first meeting with her at a reception, and the kick on the shin Penny had given him when she had seen him do a double take watching her walk across the room.

This morning she was all business, a total professional.

"Okay, first impressions. She hasn't been there long. I suppose you already sussed that, Jordan?"

Jordan nodded. "We were just lucky that she washed up against the statue."

"Yes, the next tide would have carried her away but that wasn't going to happen. This place has visitors even in the middle of winter, so it wasn't ever going to be long before she was seen. Thank goodness."

"Okay, we'll get off. We'll see you this afternoon. Come on then, Terry."

Jordan put his empty cup in a plastic bag to take with him back to the car. As they passed the coroner's van, he stopped.

"You should have a look, Terry. It's different seeing them at this stage, rather than back at the morgue."

He heard Terry Denn gasp beside him.

"Get busy, it's the best way to deal with it. Come on, we'll go back, set up a room, start our books. She hasn't been dead long, that's lucky. We have a few hours now that are golden. Let's make the most of them. First thing is to identify her."

Jordan pointed towards a bulky figure at the edge of the grassy verge.

"Go over and have a word with that bloke over there. He's in charge of all of this lot. Make sure he knows we have taken this on and we're at Wavertree. I don't want information doing the rounds to the local bods before it gets to us and wasting valuable time. Get the fingerprint images sent to us as soon as possible and any meaningful finds. Probably won't be any and I don't expect she'll be on the system, but you never know. Come on, move yourself."

Chapter 3

Ben Harwood was sweating with the effort of cleaning. There shouldn't have been so much blood. There shouldn't have been any blood. This mess wasn't part of the plan. None of this was part of the plan. If she hadn't struggled and fought back and if he hadn't screwed up there would have been none at all. It had seemed so simple and now look. He was just meant to scare her, warn her off, send her away with it clear what would happen if she came back.

But she'd been stronger than he thought she would be, a little woman like that. And she fought hard. Instead of listening to him, terrified and awed, she'd panicked and begun to fight, and she saw his face. She recognised him from the online publicity pictures. He saw it in her eyes. He should have worn a balaclava, but he'd had the scarf and the hoody. Okay, okay, he'd cocked it up good and proper. But now, he'd deal with it.

He knew that it would be impossible to get rid of the traces completely. Now, he'd have to sell the bloody van, wouldn't he? He didn't want to. It was a good van. He had seen it on the films though, even if it looked clean, even though it reeked of bleach and he'd scrubbed and hosed and mopped, evidence would still be there, trapped in the joints and corners. Just waiting to drop him right in it.

He roared and flung the long-handled brush at the wall. It didn't break, it bounced away and clattered feebly to the floor. He leaped down from the rear cargo door and kicked out at the bucket and the bottles lying around the lock-up. He probably should have left her there, on the floor in her house but then she would have been found, and they might have discovered evidence to link him to it. Definitely better to take her away.

When he left, it had looked okay, no obvious sign of the struggle, no blood, no prints. He'd been really careful about that. There had been no sign of a break-in, that part had worked well. Those old windows, so easy to lever upwards. There was nothing to raise suspicion – he replayed it in his head. No, it was fine, he'd pulled down the window, and locked the back door before he left and pushed the key through the letter box. There was nothing to make it seem other than she had just gone, done a runner.

This was supposed to have been a clean job. Easy. He had planned it all out. Right from the start. It had taken time. He'd been clever and drawn her in right up to the final phase. But now, nothing had gone the way it should have done. He sat in the driver's seat and lit up a ciggie. He'd have to up the price. If he was going to sell his van, then it was going to cost. Unforeseen expenses, that's what that was, and it shouldn't be up to him to cover them.

He nodded to himself and began to gather together the bits and pieces. Might as well get on with it, the sooner it was gone the better. He'd buy something new, when he got the extra money. Maybe a pickup – one of those big American jobs. Yeah. Look on the bright side.

He threw his few belongings into a plastic crate. There wasn't much but he wondered if it was safe to keep any of it. There was all this science now, he'd seen *CSI* and *Silent Witness*. He didn't want to come unstuck because there was some residue or whatever it was called. To be safe it should all be ditched – burned would be best, he could sort that. Not his phone though, that had been in his pocket under his sweat-shirt and his hoody so that had to be okay. His wallet, that was okay. He hadn't been stupid, that'd been locked in the glove box. So really it was just the empty Coke cans from the back, the bits of paper – his scarf, just to be on the safe side, the hat and gloves and the other thing. The cans and paper would go in a bin, any bin it didn't matter whose. The gloves and stuff, he'd burn them at Dan's allotment. No chance his mate would be going up there for a few weeks yet and there were always people with fires in old oil cans. Yes, sorted.

He bent and picked up the big metal torch. He'd been smart, he'd wrapped it in a Tesco bag straight after. He screwed up his face. Actually, he probably should have ditched it before now, and the bag. That was from the woman's house. It'd have to go in the river, that way it'd never be found. Couldn't do it now though, not in daylight you never knew who might be watching and there were cameras everywhere. Tonight, he'd get rid. Her computer could go into the canal on his way home and her phone.

Should he wash the torch? It was pretty messy, there was blood and that other stuff. He tried not to think about that – he knew what it was but if he didn't name it then it wasn't so bad. What a cock-up it had all turned into. Perhaps he'd just rinse it under the tap outside. That way even if someone saw it there'd be no fuss.

He would let the client know. Ha – client – fancy him having a client. He'd call the bloke, tell him the job was done and it was time to pay the second instalment, but it would be more money, quite a lot more. If he started asking questions, he'd blag his way through it. He'd say it was unprofessional to discuss details. Like someone in a film. Probably the bloke wouldn't ask anyway. He wouldn't want to know. He'd just be happy it was over, that the threat had gone away.

The tide would be out by now, and the biggest problem washed away so in spite of the issues with the van and the 'weapon', everything was under control. He ran water from the outside tap over the metal and then let it run and run until all the blood had gone, he even washed out the bag. No trace left, couldn't be. He wrapped one of his car cleaning towels over the Tesco bag and pushed the whole lot to the back of his storage cupboard. He'd come back later and take it down to the docks, somewhere quiet, and he'd fling it in. He smiled. Yeah that would be the best place. There must be plenty of lost tools and equipment down there so even if it was ever found, it wouldn't matter. No-one would connect it with the woman. Yeah, actually he'd made the right decision. He'd done good.

He locked up the small garage, took his racing bike and set off. He'd call in the car showrooms – have a look at some vans. Might as well enjoy it, seeing as he was going to have to change it anyway. He'd get an idea of the prices, so he'd know how much to ask for. He glanced at his watch. The bloke would be expecting a call. He'd leave it a while yet. Let him sweat a bit; the more nervous he was the more amenable he'd be to an increase in the second amount. If he kicked up a bit then he'd have to let it go, but it was worth a try.

He still had to ring work as well. He'd tell them he wouldn't be available for a few days. Being based at home made it so much easier. There wouldn't be a problem, he'd just say his sciatica was acting up again. In fact, he might as well take the rest of the week off. It'd be more convincing.

So, car showrooms and then the pub for a bevvy. Okay, things hadn't gone quite as he'd hoped but it was okay. Just some last bits to tidy up but it was all okay.

Chapter 4

Jordan scanned the room. It was small, a bit scruffy and short of tech equipment. It would do.

"Right, Terry, get on to the IT department. We need some computers set up in here. We need some more chairs, at least one for each desk, and we need two whiteboards. I'm going to have a word with the DCI and find out what sort of team we're going to have and what sort of funding we can rely on. Probably not much. We need books to be started and we need a name to be generated. They'll do that for you down in IT if you ask them. See if you can blag a kettle and some cups. This is going to be home for a while now. Hopefully not for long but let's make the best of it. Can you do all that?"

"Yes, boss."

Jordan smiled at him as he turned and left the room. The youngster was making a good start. Then he stopped in the corridor. Had he really just thought of Terry as 'the youngster'? Christ, what did that make him?

Jordan had led a couple of cases before but never a murder. Now, this was his chance to show that he could handle a major crime, start to finish. He'd need a team but wasn't sure how much he could rely on Cross to back him up. He would have to wait and see. He smiled. It was exciting and he was going to sort it. He owed it to the poor woman dumped by the tide, and he owed it to himself.

He knocked at the DCI's office door and entered. Richard Cross sat at his desk, arms folded in front of him. "Right, what do you know?" he asked.

"Young woman. Found in a plastic bin bag, caught on the legs of one of the Gormley statues. Blunt trauma to the head. Dressed in nightclothes. We are waiting for fingerprints and DNA from the medical examiner so that we can move forward with identification."

"What do you need from me?"

"I'm setting up an incident room. I need computer experts or clerical assistants with computer skills at least and some civilians for collating and manning the phones. I think we are going to have to appeal to the public for help with ID. At the moment we have no idea where she was put into the river. I need to find out about tides and tables. I think there will be someone at the university I can speak to, but I think our best bet is going to be if someone recognises her. I was hoping to have a television appeal and something in the Echo and maybe the national papers."

"Okay. You can have a small team of civilians, one of them clerical, and computers. Probably two uniforms to help with house-to-house or what have you. You've got Terry Denn. I reckon that'll do."

"So, three uniforms? Is that all."

"Two. You've got Terry Denn. I'll find you one more."

There was so much Jordan wanted to say. It was impossible to know at this stage whether that would be enough support. It certainly didn't sound like it, but Richard Cross pushed back his chair, pulled down his uniform jacket and moved across the room towards his window.

"Keep me informed. Good luck with it."

The interview was over.

***

"Operation Plover, sir." Terry Denn looked slightly bemused and embarrassed. "What's a plover?"

Jordan bit back a smile.

"It's a bird. Right, what's the situation with computers and whatnot?"

"Tomorrow at the earliest. I've got some chairs and…" He paused. "Will it be okay if I bring in a kettle from home? My mam's got a spare."

"That'd be great. Don't let anyone know though. It won't be approved."

Jordan could tell that the young detective was disappointed with the ramshackle way things were being pulled together. But he wasn't new to the force. He was fully aware, as they all were, of the financial constraints and it was encouraging that he was so willing to compromise.

"Come on, Terry. We need to move if we're going to get over to the morgue. Dr O'Connor won't wait for us. While we're there, if you think you're going to throw up or even worse pass out, leave the room. It's more dignified than landing on the floor."

"Yes, boss. Boss?"

"Yeah."

"Your first. Did you… well I mean… were you okay?"

Jordan paused for a minute and then he grinned.

"Just made it to the bog in time."

Chapter 5

There was nothing on the BBC page, nothing on the local news feeds and nothing in Twitter or Facebook. The longer he scrolled and searched, the more it seemed to Graham Matthews that the phone call had been another scam. He wasn't going to be taken in this time, no way. He began to relax.

It was lunch time and he could go for a walk around the shops. He'd go down to the landing stage, watch the tourists taking selfies with the Beatles statue. It always made him feel a bit superior. All those people coming to see his city. The wind blowing off the river would clear his head. He swiped the recent calls list. Even though the number didn't show he wanted to erase any record from his phone. He couldn't actually block it – he wanted to, oh yes, but he knew it would torment him.

Then again, perhaps the best thing would be to change his number. That way, in time, he'd forget all about this crap. Trouble with that was, it was his work phone. How would he explain that to Mr Blackwell? Even if he told the boss that he'd lost the phone he couldn't expect him to accept that he needed a new number. If he said that he was getting nuisance calls he would probably be told to suck it up and deal with them.

There was something else though.

Even though he had now decided that this was a scam, and nothing further was going to happen. There was just the possibility, still, that it wasn't. At the centre of all of this was that little nub of truth. That was why he had been taken in. Surely though, that nasty little secret from so long ago, the thing he had thought was gone from everyone's memory, couldn't have developed into this. On sleepless nights, when he was caught unprepared, he remembered. When he remembered, there came fear, along with the terrible shame.

Now and then there would be something on the news that would crawl into his head and sit there, stealing his peace. All this stuff with his wife. The IVF procedures, that hadn't helped. It had all been so emotional. Once, just once, he had come very close to telling Rose the truth. Thank God he hadn't, it would have been mad, and it would have been cruel. He saw that now.

His palms were sweating again. He really needed to deal with this better. He could either ignore it, pretend it had never happened or – the other thing. He could find out who was doing this. Maybe this was fate showing him that really, he should do something. Now that Rose was pregnant, he didn't want anything spoiling the joy. No worries about the past, no guilt. Perhaps he should try and find out, but how and where? He hadn't a clue. Apart from that, was he strong enough? Could he face what he might find?

Yes, of course he could.

His phone rang again. Another withheld number.

"Matthews," he answered.

"Don't hang up. That won't help."

"Look, I know what's going on here. I know this is a scam. You fooled me once, but if you ring this number again, I'm going to the police. In fact, I might just do that anyway. I'm warning you."

"I don't think you want to do that. I told you, the job's done. It didn't go as smoothly as I would have hoped but you owe me. You need to pay your debts."

"I don't believe you. I'm going to block your calls."

"Is that right? Well, watch your incoming messages, watch for a JPEG and then you'll see, that would be a mistake. I'll ring you tomorrow and we'll make the arrangements. You don't want to go back on the deal. Not now, not with what I know."

Graham sat at his desk with the phone in his hand. All ideas of a walk by the Pier Head, a breath of air, left him. All he wanted to do was curl into a ball in the corner of his office, to crouch like a kid in the corner and tell himself that nobody could see him.

Chapter 6

Ben's finger hovered over the send button. The trouble was that once he sent this image, it was out there. The police made short work of internet tracing. He thought it was probably an interesting job, maybe in another life he might have enjoyed a job like that. Having the freedom to surf wherever you liked without needing to worry. They probably used the dark web all the time and didn't have to hide it.

Anyway, if he set up a new email address, got yet another phone and used that, he'd be golden, especially if it wasn't a new one. One with an account attached to it. Something to cause confusion. A smile crept across his face. He glanced around the bar. It wasn't very busy but there were some who looked like regulars in there, they weren't a good bet. He might come back in one day and be recognised. There were a couple of blokes who looked as though they were having a meeting and then a gang of youngsters in the corner by the fake fireplace. He ordered a fresh pint of lager. Strolled over to where they were sprawled across the settees, their feet up on the tables.

He put his glass on the mantle and leaned towards the flickering gas flames, rubbing his hands together, blowing on his fingers. They didn't want him there, he could tell, he was invading their space. He felt the tension start to rise. He picked up his glass and took a drink.

"Alright, mate," the one nearest to the fire addressed him. "Do you want to move over like. We was here first."

"Just getting warm," Ben said.

"Just do it somewhere else, yeah."

The lad had risen now and taken the single step to close the space between them.

"Back off, la, yeah. Just wind your neck in," Ben said.

It was quicker than he had anticipated; it started with a push and then a push back and then a short ineffectual punch. One of the girls squealed, Ben wasn't sure whether it was fear or excitement, but it was just what he needed.

"Your bird's just wet herself," he said.

They rose as one now, the rest of them, shouting and pushing and kicking. The landlord was there in moments. In his hand he held an old-fashioned policeman's truncheon. Not threatening enough to be banned as a weapon, especially as it was usually mounted over the bar as decoration. He banged it on the table. There was a moment of silence. He glared at them. Ben raised his hands.

"Okay, okay."

He pushed through the little crowd of lads who were now laughing and mocking. He tripped on the table leg, steadied himself with a hand sliding on the wooden top and then stood to glower at them all.

With a final expletive he stormed from the pub. It wasn't his local, he'd leave it a while before he went in there again. He pushed his hand in his pocket, jogged across the road and jumped onto the bus that had just pulled into the stop. By the time the lad noticed that his phone had gone from the table, Ben was on his way home. Once there, he took the SD card out of his phone and slotted it into the stolen one. He copied the file into the phone storage then removed the card and, once it was back in his own phone, he deleted the picture.

He deleted all the other images from the stolen phone. He wouldn't risk sending the wrong one, he knew how easily that might happen. It was possible the lad had a tracer on it, so he removed the battery and stowed the handset in a drawer. He would wait until the next morning, take it somewhere else, send the image and then throw the phone away. It would do that Matthews bloke good to sweat for a bit. Ben grinned when he thought of him, constantly looking at his phone, waiting and dreading the tone telling him there was a message. The loser, he was only getting what he deserved after all.

He wouldn't look at it again for now. He didn't like to think about what had happened in too much detail. It wasn't supposed to have been like that. Stupid bitch, she shouldn't have struggled, she shouldn't have seen him. Okay, he held his hands up to it – the thing had gone wrong – but it was over now, and he expected to be paid. Then it was finished. He would learn from it. He needed a bit of time before he did anything like this again. Next time it would be better, he'd be more well prepared. Yes, he'd benefitted from the experience and next time he'd do better.

He'd learned a lot. He'd known already that people were mugs, but it was amazing just how stupid they could be. The girl had told him everything he needed. Just because he put the questions on a form with the company name at the top she'd not held back. Name, address – even changed that when she moved – bank card details. That had been clever, *No payment will be taken until the trace is complete*. That made her feel safe. Of course, he couldn't have taken payment, not with a fake form and email address. But she'd been so open, giving him far more information than he really needed.

Chapter 7

Terry did well. As the Y incision was made, and the internal organs were removed and weighed, he stood firm, resolute and unblinking. Even as the victim's face was peeled downwards the young detective just nodded as Phil dictated into the microphone above her head.

Back in the incident room Jordan made them both coffees. Terry had slumped onto a desk chair. None of the others spoke, though a couple of them glanced at him and grimaced.

"There you are, Terry. You did okay, mate."

Before the other detective was forced to respond, Jordan turned away and moved to where they had positioned the whiteboards. He addressed the newly gathered team.

"Okay, the victim was a young, healthy woman. She had no obvious disease, no harm caused by drugs or alcohol abuse, though of course we will wait for the toxicology reports to confirm that, and she had eaten a couple of hours just before she died. Stomach contents were partly digested salmon, vegetables and some apple."

It was that relatively mild comment that proved a bridge too far. He'd watched the contents poured into a container, but now, as the findings were related, the memory of them proved too much. Terry rose quickly from his chair, hand over his mouth, and ran from the room. The civilians looked down at their desks. The young, uniformed officer who had been assigned to the team, Rosalind Searle, made a sympathetic face, but the older bloke who was setting up the computers, turned back to the others with a grin.

"Ah well," he said, "better out than in, I reckon."

A few minutes later Terry came back; the front of his hair was wet, and his freckles were stark against pale skin, but he smiled as he sat down.

Jordan nodded at him and turned to the boards.

"Right then. Let's see what we've got. Death was the result of blunt trauma to the head. That's no surprise. We have no weapon and until we identify this poor girl, we have no chance of finding a motive. Unless we are incredibly lucky with the house-to-house there is very little possibility that we'll find our killer. We have a small team of uniformed officers culled from the shift in the morning. Tomorrow we do a house-to-house once the reports have been in the papers."

He turned towards the four civilians.

"And that is when you guys will be able to help us most. We are going to need someone to collate and keep the records in order. There will be response sheets and hopefully phone calls. Who's going to take that on?" He waited for a moment, but no-one volunteered. "Could you do that, please?"

He gestured to a middle-aged woman with short curly hair and narrow glasses with black frames.

"You are?"

"Beverly Powell. Call me Bev, sir."

"Excellent. So, can everyone make sure Bev has a record of all the calls and follow-ups and anything that you think is important. She will report back to us. We don't know each other very well as yet but we need to hit the ground running. The media liaison department have already put together a statement for the Echo and the free papers and there will be news reports tonight. So, I want two of you to stay late and the rest to come in early tomorrow ready to go. Sort it out between you. Don't exhaust yourselves because we are probably going to put in some long hours for the next few days. Any questions?"

There were none.

"Okay, Terry, you and me are going back to the beach. We'll make a start on the house-to-house, just the ones closest to the scene and we'll see if there are any joggers, dog walkers, metal detector people – what do you call them?"

"Don't know, sir. Weirdos?"

Jordan turned away to hide the smile.

Chapter 8

They spent a couple of hours canvassing the houses near the beach. Everyone they interviewed knew what had happened and most of them had questions, but nobody could give them any new information, except for a gang of lads who said they'd seen a van the night before. Unfortunately, they couldn't agree on the size, the colour, the time they had seen it, or how long it had been there.

"I know we've already requested CCTV footage from the area, but tomorrow let's make sure everyone knows about this van," Jordan said. "It's more than likely just a delivery man, they work late, or perhaps just someone come down for a walk on the beach. Realistically, the possibility of the murderer being here is pretty remote anyway. Unless, by some chance, he knew the body had washed up. We are pretty sure she came down with the tide. No, this is not going to get us very far, but we have to show that we did it. We might as well call it a day. We need a breakthrough, and quickly. We need to ID our victim."

They were back at the car. Jordan stripped off his jacket, throwing it onto the back seat.

"Right, Terry. Check first thing in the morning whether anything has come in from the Misper list or the news bulletins. They were working to present a computer-generated image. Given that she was in nightwear. A decent dressing gown, a pretty nighty; I don't think this was a homeless woman, not a rough sleeper or someone running away. This was someone taken from her home, either dead or alive and we won't get any further until we find out where her home was. I'll see you in the morning, Terry."

* * *

It didn't take Jordan long to drive the short distance to his own home and when he arrived, the house was in darkness. It was just after ten. Penny had obviously given up on him getting back in time for dinner and called it a day. There was a dish of chilli and rice in the microwave and a bottle of red wine on the kitchen counter. She had left a note to let him know that she had a job interview in the morning and her sister would be looking after Harry.

Jordan ate his meal but ignored the wine. He was already half asleep. He went into the nursery and leaned over the cot. His son was sleeping. As Jordan leaned to kiss his head, the baby stirred and mumbled. The big eyes opened, and the little boy's lip quivered. Jordan reached in and picked him up. The last thing they needed now was a disturbed night. He rocked Harry, humming quietly to him as he took him out onto the landing to stand and gaze through the small window.

After a while, he felt the weight in his arms change as the baby drifted back to sleep and his breathing deepened. Once Harry was back in his cot, Jordan undressed in the bathroom. He didn't run the shower. The noise would wake his wife. It would do in the morning. Penny was on her back, her hair a dense, dark cloud across the pillow, the covers pulled up to her chin. He slid under the duvet and lay as still as he could, listening to his wife breathe. She turned and mumbled in her sleep and he moved closer and put an arm around her. The trees outside were blowing in the rising wind, shadows played on the walls dulled and mishappen by the lightweight curtains. A dog barked somewhere close by and there was the roar of a motor bike in the distance. He felt calm and happy. He had a large boisterous extended family but these two souls, his wife, and his boy, were what mattered. As long as they were safe and well, he could deal with the ugliness outside.

Somewhere, there was another house, another bed, it was cold and empty now and there was yet another where someone sheltered who had taken a life and thrown the body into the Mersey. Could they sleep or would their dreams be tortured by the thing that they had done? He would ask them. When he found them and brought them in, he would ask them.

Chapter 9

Jordan was awake early. Harry and Penny were just stirring as he left the house, pulling his collar up against the cold. He was fired up and ready to go. It was still too early for the café and he was grateful for Terry's mum's kettle.

Before she left the night before, Bev had sorted the records from the phone calls into two piles labelled 'Promising' and 'Probably a waste of time'.

He started with the 'Promising' ones. A couple were hopeful calls from people with missing relatives and, though he would need to go through them, he thought it unlikely that their victim was someone who had been missing from home. Those would wait for now. He ended up with a little pile that were of definite interest. Three people had given the same suggestion.

Beatrice Sharp.

A woman had called from a printing company in the city to say that the woman in the photo looked very much like their new secretary. A bloke who ran a convenience store thought it might be one of his customers. Then there was a neighbour. A woman who thought she recognised her as a tenant at a flat in Kirkby. She didn't know her, but she'd seen her on the bus, said hello, and talked about the weather. Hadn't seen her for a few weeks though.

It was too early to call anyone back, so he logged onto Facebook and entered the name, Beatrice Sharp. He discounted the ones based outside of the UK, for now at least. Two were in London and one in Liverpool. It had been too much to hope for – one glance at the profile picture showed him that this middle-aged woman, surrounded by children wasn't the Beatrice that they were looking for.

He put the papers on Terry's desk with a short note: *Arrange interviews. Meet me in town at the printers. Keep me informed.*

* * *

The woman from the printing company was convinced that the girl they were looking for was their new secretary. The picture on her HR file was as much confirmation as they needed.

Jordan couldn't wipe the grin from his face as they went back to the cars to drive to the address they'd been given.

"Bloody hell, Terry, I can't believe this. Don't let this fool you," Jordan said. "We're not usually so lucky. Normally we have to spend days and days talking to people who believe Elvis works in their chippy and John Lennon is hiding in a flat at the Albert Dock."

Jordan's head was reeling with tide tables and highwater times. When he was back in the office later, he would need to go through the notes again. Basically, he already understood that the body could have been carried from any of number of points on the riverbank, from built-up areas, riverside parks and of course, and what seemed more likely, secluded spots down narrow paths. There was no way they could investigate all of them so, unless they were unbelievably lucky, there wasn't a lot of point following that line of enquiry. He put it to one side for the time being.

This was more promising. There was a convenience store consisting of a small supermarket with a post office in the corner. "We'll pop in there, see if they know our victim. Find out if she was seen with anyone regularly," Jordan said.

The roads in the area were lined with small semidetached homes or short terraces, low rise flats, and in the distance, there were a couple of tower blocks. It wasn't run-down. The houses were typical of so many built in the sixties and seventies, but it was unlovely.

"I don't know this area," Jordan said.

"Ah well, I know it," Terry answered. "I live not far from here. Over the other side, in Southdene. This part is Westvale. I live with my mam."

"Oh…" Jordan fought to find a positive response.

"It's not as bad as it used to be. Not too many torched cars these days. Me, Nan and Granda were moved here from Brownlow Hill, in the city, down by the cathedral, the Anglican one. Now the old ones have gone there's just me and her. I've got a brother, Paul, but he lives in Spain with his partner; he's gay. Mam tries, but she struggles with the idea of it all. Anyway, one day I intend to move us out. When I'm earning enough. At the moment we're in the house Granda bought with Margaret Thatcher's scheme. They're hard to sell, tainted by the 'council house history'."

"I didn't know that you lived here," Jordan said.

"No, to be honest it's not an address you brag about. But as I say, it's not as bad as it used to be. A lot of people have bought their own houses now, it makes a difference, gives them a stake you know." Terry laughed. "There is one thing though."

"Yeah?"

"Community. That's always been strong in these places. Maybe sometimes it's made things difficult for us – you know, *the job*. But it's special. I don't think you get it so much anymore, in other places, like."

Jordan glanced around him; there was a small gang of lads on bikes at the end of the road. They were just standing about, watching, but he wasn't sure he'd want to meet them on his own at night. Community spirit or not.

* * *

The shopkeeper took the picture in his hand and shook his head.

"She was lovely, didn't live around here very long. She came a few times a week. She bought bread and bacon, eggs that sort of thing and sometimes wine. We would talk, in the evening when it was quiet. She told me her name. Not very usual these days, but I had an Aunt Beatrice and everyone called her Bea. Ms Sharp said I could call her Bea if I wanted. She's nice. I can't believe anyone would hurt her. I hope that's not her but to be honest it looks so much like her; I reckon it is."

The shopkeeper described the victim, height, hair colour, general appearance. He looked again at the computer-generated image and nodded.

"She was pretty, so young and pleasant to talk to," he said. "She said she wouldn't be staying long. She'd just taken a flat here to put her on until she found something more permanent. You can't blame her really I suppose, if you're single with no ties."

They promised they would let him know when they were sure of the woman's identity, but they all knew they were empty words. They had found their victim.

Next, they walked to the small block of flats. They climbed the two flights of concrete stairs to the small square landing. The bell didn't seem to be working and they knocked on the glass panel in the front door. A young woman with a baby straddling her hip leaned through the window of the adjacent flat. "She's gone."

"Sorry." Jordan showed her his warrant card. "Do you know the woman who lives here."

"Lived. Like I say. She's gone. Only there a few weeks. Didn't even bring her own furniture."

"So, it's rented?"

"Aye."

"Do you know who handles it?"

"What am I – bloody Google?" She jigged the fractious child up and down for a minute. "Sorry, no sleep. Yeah, it's that place in the precinct. The one with the blue door. Bloke called Steve."

"Thanks, love." The window slammed shut.

"Get onto that will you, Terry."

Chapter 10

Ben stared at his screen. He couldn't breathe. His heart pounded. This wasn't true. It couldn't be. He grabbed the remote and switched off the TV. Then he turned it on again – it was still there, a computer-generated image of the girl. There, filling all fifty-five inches. Okay it wasn't a photograph, it was a drawing really, but it was her. It was her, completely, but not as he last saw her. Not bleeding out on the floor with a hole in her skull. Not her with her eyes closed. He'd had to close her eyes. Here on the television staring down at him. Her hair was loose, flowing down over her shoulders, not clumped and wet with all that stuff.

He felt his stomach heave, he felt saliva fill his mouth and before he had a chance to move he had thrown up all over his knee, vomit running down his jeans, over his chin, in the mug that he'd been holding. He screwed up his eyes. Tried to get his breath but his stomach revolted again, and he had to run for the bathroom.

When the puking stopped, and his eyes had cleared, and the gasping and gulping eased, he pushed himself up using the toilet bowl to lean on. The tiles were disgusting, and he felt foul, covered in partly digested curry. He peeled off his clothes and threw them into the corner, turned on the shower and climbed into the tub.

He was shaking from head to toe. For a long time, all he could do was stand with his forehead leaning against the walls, holding himself up with braced arms, letting the water run over his body. The panic was complete, a red fugue that he couldn't get through.

Once his breathing had calmed, he pulled back the shower curtain. The room was a mess, Mam would be livid. So, he clambered out and wrapped himself in the big bath sheet. He picked up his clothes and retched again. The room was spinning and he had to sit on the lavatory for a minute. He wrapped the jeans and top together and carried them carefully down to the back kitchen and stuck them into the washer. He wasn't sure what setting it should be on, his mam did this stuff, but he twiddled the knobs and put a tablet in. If the clothes were ruined, it didn't matter, he would fling them.

Back in the bathroom he cleaned up as much as he could, he used the spray cleaner and sloshed water around. By the time she was back from the bingo it should have dried. If she asked, then he'd just tell her he'd had a bad curry and he felt really grotty and she'd come over all sympathetic and probably make him drink Lucozade or whatever. But that was okay. Right now, someone taking care of him, fussing over him would be lovely.

He went back into the lounge and stared at the big screen. The reports had moved on. He knew he was going to have to find out what had happened, but he couldn't – not this way. He just couldn't see that girl's face looking down at him. Bigger than life. He turned it off.

He pulled out his phone and logged onto the internet. He found the Liverpool Echo website and read with growing horror the report of the discovery on the beach at Crosby.

He was screwed. This was never supposed to happen. No, this couldn't be.

The idea had been simple. He was just going to scare her, show her what he could do and then, at the last minute let her go. But it wasn't as easy as he thought it would be. She had kicked and wriggled and dragged at the plastic bag. He had thought that it would slip over her head, quick and easy – it always did in films. But it didn't. It had been too small, it had caught on her ears and slowed him down. She'd got her hands to it and ripped it. She'd screamed, and in the end, there had been no choice but to hit her with the torch. She'd seen him, she would be able to identify him. He'd hit her over and over, scared and shocked he'd lost his mind until she lay on the floor bleeding. Then he'd had to clear it all up, the mess and the body, find a bag, dump it. Let the river have her. But the river didn't want her. The river had pushed her onto the sands and left her to be found and now he didn't know what to do.

Chapter 11

Terry was reading from his notebook. He'd brought them a Greggs pasty at the shops and Jordan was attempting to nibble at the meat and veggies and avoid the fatty pastry, but the thing smelled so good, he was struggling. He screwed up the bag and tossed it into a waste bin.

"I've spoken to the estate agents. Beatrice rented short term. The place is furnished, and they prefer anything to nothing, so she had it on a month-to-month. They didn't bother with following up her references. She paid a month in advance and the bloke said he could tell by looking at her that she was 'a decent sort'. She paid in cash and that didn't set off any alarms. Apparently, it's not that unusual in the area. People who can't get credit or even bank accounts. They borrow the money and there's no way to trace it back. Turned out she was there a few weeks and then moved on. I've got a forwarding address which was a surprise, but it seems it's one thing they insist on, in case there's damage or whatever. It's in Walton, let's hope it's genuine."

* * *

The house in Walton was part of a small terrace. The front door opened directly onto the street. The small window was covered by a blind. Terry pressed his face against the glass but could see nothing. Jordan hammered with the small brass knocker and then stepped back to look up at the bedroom windows. There was no response. He knocked again and thumped with the side of his fist against the wood. There was a bad-tempered shout from the house next door.

"What the hell is all this row?" An old man peered at them from around the door frame. "Stop that bloody racket. I haven't even got my hearing aid in and I can hear you."

Jordan held up his warrant card. "DI Jordan Carr. We're looking for the woman who lives here."

"Why? What's she done?"

"We don't know that she's done anything. We are concerned about her welfare. Do you know her?"

"You'll have to speak up."

The man held a hand cupped around his ear. Jordan tried again, louder.

"Do you know her?"

"What's it got to do with you who I know?" The door began to close. Terry held up a hand and stepped across.

"Aw right, granda. We're just tryin' to find her. Just want a quick word."

Jordan noted how the young DC altered his diction, just slightly, just enough to change the expression on the face of the old man from suspicion to mild irritation. But it was enough to stop him going back inside.

"Well, you can leave her alone. She's a smashing girl. Not been here long but she's helped me out with me shopping." He wagged a finger at Terry. "You don't want to be upsettin' people. Just leave her alone. Haven't you got some motorists to annoy?"

"When did you see her last?" Terry said.

The old man sighed, pulled the door a little wider and stepped into the space. In spite of himself he was enjoying the attention.

"Now then, let me see. Last week, I saw her on Thursday. She took a flutter down to BetFred for me. I wasn't so good on me pins last week. I saw her going off to work, regular as clockwork she is, anyway I had a quick word. I don't sleep and so I watch out, see everybody going off, watch for postie. Not that he ever brings me anything these days. Ha, nothing except the bloody bills, he brings them alright. Anyway, didn't win so I didn't expect her coming back in the evening. And she didn't."

"Did you see her on Friday?"

"Aye, I did. Saw her Friday and Saturday, off into town on Saturday all dollied up. Nice though, not slutty."

"Monday?" Jordan had moved to join them. A nosy neighbour was a policeman's best friend. "Or did you see anyone else? A visitor maybe?"

"No, now as you mention it, not Monday. Should have done, I was watching out. That lad from across the road had his bloody bike out, rattling and banging. Early that was, about half seven. So, I would have seen her. She usually gives me a wave. But no, didn't see her. Visitors? No, never see her have no visitors."

"Thanks a lot, mate. Are you okay, like? Do you need anything?" Terry asked.

"Aye, I want you to bugger off and leave us in peace."

Jordan pulled out the picture of the woman and held it for the old man to peer at.

"Is this her, is this your neighbour?"

"Aye, that's her. I'll tell you though, if you're going to try and pin something on her you're on a hiding to nothing. She's a lovely woman."

From inside there came the blare of the television.

"That's my race." And the door was slammed as the old man went back to his living room.

They walked to the end of the small terrace where a narrow passage led to the back of the houses. The entrances were all locked and bolted and they counted dwellings as they passed. Beatrice's place was fifth in the line and when Jordan rattled the old wooden gate it swung open into a paved yard. A washing line was strung across the area, a pair of trousers hung damp and dejected on the rope. A couple of buckets were lying on their sides by the back door and an old crate stood near the sash window. The top was broken down but apart from that there was no sign of disturbance. Jordan looked through the narrow pane. He nodded once.

"We need SOCO down here. There's no sign of life. One cup on the draining board, one chair beside the table. She lived here alone. Make the call will you, Terry?"

Chapter 12

Ben's mam fussed and fretted over him. She was annoyed about the mess and stink in the bathroom, but she was a mother first and foremost and she had to take care of her boy. She made him warm lemonade and tucked him into bed and stroked his forehead as if he were a schoolboy.

He should have felt comforted, normally he would lap it up, the pampering, but tonight he just wanted her to go away and leave him be. He turned onto his side, closed his eyes, and lay quietly until he heard her close the bedroom door and the soft sound of her feet on the stairs.

He pulled out his phone and logged back onto the news feeds. It was everywhere, the pictures of the girl, the images of the little group on the beach. They still didn't know who she was. '*Ongoing enquiries*' the police said. Then there was the usual promise that they would find who had committed this terrible crime and bring them to justice. His stomach lurched again, and he tasted bile in his mouth.

He took in some deep breaths. He had to get away. The police weren't total numpties. They weren't super sleuths, not like the ones in the American films, not like the rebel detectives who went out and brilliantly solved cases. No, he knew it wasn't like that but still, they had all this technology now and his own knowledge was lacking. Okay, he had cleaned and cleared what he could. He'd taken precautions beforehand, but he didn't know if it was enough.

He went through it all again and the more he thought about it the more convinced he was that, for the time being he would be okay. They didn't even know who she was. Even when they found that out, and there was no use kidding himself, that would be easy for them – a piece of piss. But there was no connection between them, not in the flesh, she'd never met him. Not until that night anyway. Then there was the river, the plastic bag. All that water washing over the bag and it would probably be torn as it had washed down with the tide and so she would be dirty and sluiced by Mersey water. There couldn't be anything of him left on her.

So, what he needed to do was to get away, but there wasn't so much of a desperate hurry. He probably had a day or two. He would be organised. A plane to Spain, then on from there, maybe over to Germany. He would ring work, tell them he wanted to take some holiday. He had a few weeks owing to him and his contract was pretty flexible. He could make it look good, say his back was playing up but he didn't want to stay on the sick. He didn't know how long he would need to be away. Play it by ear, that was it. So, he needed money. Cash – now.

He took out the new burner phone, one of several that he'd picked up from a stall in St John's Market. See, he wasn't stupid, he had known that there would be a need to make contact, anonymous calls. He dialled Graham Matthews. When he answered, the man was edgy, nervous. Of course, he probably knew who was calling, an unknown number.

"Have you seen the news?" Ben asked.

"Who is this?"

"Don't play silly buggers. You know who this is. Have you seen the news?" Ben said.

"Yes."

"So?"

"What do you mean? I don't understand." Graham was hesitant, puzzled.

"The girl," Ben said.

"Which girl?"

"Oh, come on. She's all over the television, all over the internet. You must have put two and two together. You can't be that stupid."

"Oh, bloody hell. No. No, you're not telling me, that's her?"

"Er hello! Two and two – surely you put them together."

"God, no. I never thought. I didn't expect… You said there'd be no fuss. I never thought you meant… When you said you'd sort it, this wasn't what I imagined."

"Oh really, what did you imagine, eh? That I'd have a nice little conversation and that would fix everything. Anyway, like I told you, things didn't go according to plan."

"Don't call me. Don't contact me. Keep away."

"Sorry, mate. That won't wash. It's too late for you to back out."

"No, no – this isn't what I expected."

"Okay, but just what did you expect?" Ben said.

"I don't know – but not this. This is huge, a nationwide hunt they said. Pulling out all the stops."

"Aye well. Seems I miscalculated, didn't I? The point is you're in the shit as much as I am."

"No, I'm not. I haven't done anything. I haven't."

"Ha. Tell that to the bizzies. You're in it up to your neck, mate. You don't expect me to take the fall for this do you? They get me and I drop you right in it. Simples."

There was silence at the other end, except for the harsh sound of fast breathing. Ben waited for a minute.

"So?"

"What are we going to do?"

"I'm going away. As you said, there's no connection between you and her, except what I know, don't forget that. I reckon, if I go away for a while, just until this all dies down, we'll both be in the clear. But don't kid yourself, I won't hesitate to dob you in if they catch me. I'll go off for a while, keep me head down and we'll be fine. Thing is though, I need money. I need money for tickets and lodgings and a bit of scratch to keep me going. So, you'll have to get some cash. I reckon about ten thou should be enough. I'll give you a call tomorrow. Mid-morning, that'll give you a chance to get it sorted and I'll tell you where to bring it."

He didn't wait, didn't want to listen to the ear bending that he knew would be coming. He needed to get organised, pack some stuff and send an email to work. He looked at his face in his dressing table mirror. He was pale and haggard, but it was okay. It was all going to be okay. Come on, they didn't even know who she was yet.

Chapter 13

The street in Walton was narrow and the SOCO van caused a bit of a fuss. In the end, the driver pulled onto the pavement. That caused another furore as people tried to squeeze past. Yes, they could have crossed over and walked down the other side but then they wouldn't have as much to complain about, and it wouldn't have given them the chance to rant at the coppers. In the end there was no option but to tape off the area around the house. Jordan had hoped to do this quietly and with as little fuss as possible. He should have known by now that it wouldn't work.

They suited up and pulled on gloves and booties. The scene of crime officers had already laid down a route into the house where they checked the laminate floor and then placed low steps to walk on.

In the kitchen the team was searching for fingerprints, hair, blood – anything that would indicate a crime had been committed. They were dismantling the drain from beneath the sink. In the corner someone was emptying a vacuum cleaner. It was so very everyday that it seemed to Jordan terribly poignant. The sign of a life being lived.

"I don't think there's any point in us hanging around here. We might as well get back and have a look at what's come in after the appeals." Jordan raised his voice. "Who's in charge, mate?"

A bulky figure kneeling on the tiles glanced up. "Sergeant Bailey, she's upstairs I think." The technician waved a hand vaguely in the direction of the hallway.

"Cheers." He turned to where Terry was crouched in the corner, examining a shelf of cookery books. "I reckon it's best to leave them to get on, Detective Constable."

He didn't want to say, 'please don't touch'. Terry surely knew that it was best if everything was left alone so that it could be photographed in place, and fully documented.

"Can you run up and tell Sergeant Bailey that we're back at Wavertree."

Outside a crowd gathered. The man from next door had fetched a kitchen chair to his step and a mug of tea. A uniformed constable remonstrated with him for a while, suggesting he'd be better in the house. But he wasn't to be shifted.

There was a group of kids hanging around who should obviously have been at school. Jordan was tempted to ring someone from youth services, but what was the point? He had other things to attend to. A couple of women leaned against the wall of the house opposite. One of them rocked a pushchair back and forth and the child inside lolled sideways, his small head bobbing with the movement.

It made him think of his own family. He would call Penny when he had a minute. She had her interview today and he should ask how it had gone. This one was with the citizens advice bureau and she was very keen. The money wasn't brilliant but the idea of helping other people was attractive to her. He didn't care what she did. If she wanted to carry on volunteering in the homeless shelter and the adult literacy scheme, it would be fine with him.

They could manage on his money, and the main thing was that she was happy and fulfilled.

He glanced across at the sleeping child. He hated the idea that his son would soon be going to a nursery, but he couldn't say that. It wasn't right for him to tell her what to do and she had spent weeks finding the right place. Next week Harry was to start, three mornings just to get him settled, and then the week after he would go for full days. Life was moving on, as it should, and after the dodgy start with Penny's postnatal problems, he was glad things were so much better now. But, his little boy, in the care of someone else. It saddened him. His mum had been there for him when he was little. In the morning when he left for school and in the evening when he came home. She'd had a job, in a shop, but she'd fitted the hours in so that she would be there for her children. Now, he realised what a sacrifice she had made.

He mustn't ever let Penny know how he felt. She should never feel guilt. She was entitled to her own life and they would make it work. It'd probably be good for Harry. Mixing, socialising – yes, it'd be good.

Terry clattered back down the stairs behind him, and they walked to the car.

"Hey, have you met that Sergeant Bailey?" he said.

"No, I don't think so."

"She had one of those suits on and all the gear, but she looks pretty fit. I wonder if she's married."

"Concentrate, Detective Constable."

"Oh yeah, 'course, it's just that…" Terry glanced around and when he saw the grin on Jordan's face, he stopped defending himself and laughed. "You're an old married man, but me…"

"Yeah, okay. But as I say, concentrate eh?"

They passed a uniformed officer carrying a clipboard, conducting the enquiry of the nearby properties. Jordan held up his warrant card.

"Anything interesting come up?"

"No, sir. Sorry. Seems that not many people were even aware of her. The house was empty for a while and then she moved in a short time ago and that's about it. Nobody knows whether it's rented or she owned it."

"Okay, keep at it. You never know."

"What do you reckon then, Terry? Was she killed here? It doesn't seem likely, there's no mess. But, if not then where – and more than that of course is, why? Come on – we need to move. We need a break, but it won't come if we don't push it. Oh yes and find out which agent handled the property."

Chapter 14

It was very early. Graham's phone was on vibrate. Since the pregnancy, Rose had been suffering badly with morning sickness and, honestly, he couldn't deal with it. So, he had been creeping out of bed without disturbing her. After a wash in the downstairs bathroom he would bring her a cup of tea and a plain biscuit, just before he left for work. It made him seem caring and thoughtful, brownie points all round, and he was on the way to the office before the puking started.

He didn't know how she coped with it, but she did. In a funny way she seemed to be pleased about it. Okay, he sort of understood, it made her feel very pregnant and, in these early days when there was just a little thickening at her waist that only he could detect, that and the increased size of her boobs, which would have been good if she hadn't complained that they were sensitive and vetoed any handling. But she welcomed this early sign of the baby. Still though, he didn't want her waking just now. He grabbed the phone and took it out onto the landing.

An unknown number. He rejected the call. Moments later it rang again, he rejected the call. But he knew, this wouldn't work and so the next time it rang, after just a few moments, he answered.

"What?"

"Well, that's not a very nice greeting, is it?"

Graham ground his teeth. He could hear his breath, snorting through his nostrils. His fists clenched. He screwed his eyes shut. He needed to take control.

"What do you want, arsehole?"

"Oh, nice. Listen, you need to take care, mate. You need to remember just who you're talking to. You need to remember just how much I can mess up your effin' life. It wouldn't take much. You were in the crap before, but now, mate, now you are so deep in that you'd never get out."

"Look just get this over. Tell me how much and I'll tell you when."

"How do you mean; you'll tell me when? That's not how it's going to work. I'm calling the shots. Anyway, I already told you another ten thou."

"Ten – that's impossible. The first five was difficult. No, I can't."

"Yes, you can. Things have hotted up. You must have watched the news. I need to get away for a while and it's not cheap. I'll ring you later to tell you where and when. For now, just organise it, yeah?"

* * *

Graham paced to the window of his office, back and forth. His stomach churned. He asked himself again. What the hell had he done?

Nothing. He hadn't actually 'done' anything. He'd spoken to someone on the phone. That was all. Some person, who called him, sent his whole life into turmoil.

Ah, but then he had given this man money. This stranger. He had put thousands of pounds into an envelope and left it in a waste bin. It would be impossible to explain that in any meaningful way. He had lied as well.

He had lied to his wife. Told her that he needed the money to pay for a repair on the car. Then he'd had to leave the car hidden for a week and rent a replacement – lies, more lies. That was going to come back and hit him on the backside in the not too distant future. They needed that money. They'd saved it together and it was earmarked, it was for the house move. His eyes filled with tears. He blinked them away. He'd let his wife down. It was only a question of time before it was all laid bare, unless he sorted this.

He'd been a fool. He could see that now. The bloke had sent a letter with the so called 'evidence' in it. He'd been taken in, panicked. Now at a couple of weeks' distance he could see what an idiot he'd been. There was supposed to be a JPEG, what had happened to that? Not that he wanted it, he couldn't bear to imagine what it might have shown. Trouble was, there was nothing he could do about it all. He couldn't tell anyone, ever. Now there were these other calls and worse, worse than anything, the pictures on the news. The pretty young woman. He gripped hold of the edge of his desk as the world swung around him. No, he mustn't go down that way. She was nothing to him. She was a stranger. Things were bad enough, there was no room for more anguish.

He'd been taken for a ride and it had cost him – cost him in money and in sleepless nights and in the rows that his ill temper had caused between him and Rose. He couldn't let it go on.

He'd work some extra hours, go out and find a few new clients, up his bonus. He was up for promotion and he would make it happen. A seat on the board, expenses, all of that. It was difficult trying to sell investments, times were hard for everyone, but he used to be able to do it. He'd let himself slide, lost the killer instinct, since he and Rose had been married. Life had been good, easy. Except for the one little fly in the ointment and they had dealt with that. She was going to be a mother. It had cost them both in money and physical discomfort, but it had worked and the look on her face when they were given the news had made all that worthwhile. She'd settled down and gone back to being the lovely, sunny woman he'd first met. The problem had turned her nasty for a while, short-tempered and mean. He hadn't realised how mean she could be, but that was all gone now. She was happy again.

Okay, he'd pay this lowlife the extra cash and he'd tell him that was the end. Any more trouble and he'd go to the police and take the consequences.

He dragged out his old notebook. He'd get back to some of his older clients, sweet-talk them into increasing their funds. Convince them with blurb about the uncertain times they were living in. Anything to make them give him more money. He'd make some calls. There must be some of them with a bit of spare cash hanging about. Times might be lean but there were always some people with a bit extra.

He sat down, put his head in his hands. It was no good. That wasn't going to cut it. It would be far too long before his bonus came through, the bloke wouldn't wait for that. He needed the money now, today or at least in the next few days.

He could increase the loan they had from the bank. The one they'd used to pay for the IVF. But then he'd have to explain to Rose.

He clicked at the computer keyboard. Opened up his client list.

Maybe… He leaned in closer. Maybe there was another way. He had a long list, a little from each account would soon mount up. Monthly payments were due – it would be a while before it was noticed if some of them were short. He could put it down to human error, or maybe not even that – a computer glitch. The foreign investment accounts would be even better, he could finagle them, the exchange rates were changing constantly. Maybe… Ten thousand though. Ten. It was a hell of a lot. He leaned in closer.

Began to jot down figures; sweat ran down his back. What had he got himself into?

Chapter 15

They had known, when the appeal on the media went out, that there would be a mixture of responses. There would be the callers who were misguided. People who thought that it was helpful to express their sadness and outrage at the loss of a young life. There were others who wanted to berate the force, the law, the government, and the royal family for the wrongs in society that had led to this. There were the regulars. People known to the police who responded to every announcement. They had always seen the victim, or the missing person, or the violent thug. These were an irritation because they couldn't be ignored. It was always possible that one of them had genuinely seen something of value and if they missed it, well they just couldn't let that happen. The media would have them lynched. Look at what happened with The Yorkshire Ripper.

There were small piles of printouts on the table by the door. Beverly was hanging around, straightening the edges, adding more.

"What are these?" Jordan asked.

"More telephone results from the appeal, sir. They are still coming in, though it's slowing a bit now. I wanted to know what to do about the online responses. Do you want me to print those out also, or maybe just forward them from the main list?"

"Christ, don't print them. We're supposed to be cutting down on paper."

"Okay. So, I've started to collate them. 'Probable waste of time', here." She laid a hand flat on the top of one pile. "'Possibles that need a follow up but not urgent', here." Again, she touched the papers. "And these…" She pointed to a much smaller pile. "These are ones that I thought you should look at. Ones that seem promising in one way or the other."

She stood back looking down at the table, her head tipped to one side.

Jordan wasn't sure how to react. He nodded.

"Okay, so…" He reached out to lift the top sheet from the pile nearest to him. "These are what you believe are a waste of time?"

"No, no. Blue are a waste of time."

"Blue?"

"There, that dot. I've catalogued them. Blue, waste of time. Yellow, need a second look and red – well – red are the ones that look useful."

"Okay. That's really…" Jordan paused, he glanced at Terry who was watching with his eyebrows raised. "That's useful. Thing is though – how did you decide which were to go into which pile?"

"It was pretty obvious to be honest."

"Did you do this on your own?"

"I did, I stayed late and then came in early. I reckoned it would be good to get straight on it – *'hit the ground running'* like you said, Detective Inspector. I've colour-coded the computer records in the same way. Flags."

"Flags?"

"Yes, sir. Flags."

"Right. Excellent. How long have you been with us, Bev?"

"Over a year, sir, but this is my first murder. I've been on crime figures up until now, and some data entry for HOLMES. I needed a change."

She smiled broadly.

"Okay – that's… great stuff. Thanks. I'll take these and go through them. I'm looking for any sightings of the victim in the days before her death. We know she was okay on Thursday but what happened after that?"

"I have highlighted the comments that seem most helpful. In green. You shouldn't have any trouble finding them."

"Green. Right – excellent."

She beamed at him. "Do you need anything else? Coffee?"

"Nope. That's lovely, thanks. I'll see to my drink."

Terry leaned across to where Jordan had begun to scan his overnight messages.

"I reckon you've scored there, boss," he said.

"Oh, shut up. She was just doing her best. Anyway, that's inappropriate." He split the pile of papers. "You can go through those. Give me a few minutes, I want to have another look at the tide tables. If we see when the tides were going out in between Saturday, when the neighbour saw her, and the body washing up on Tuesday, we might have an idea when she was thrown in. That might help us with where. I don't hold out much hope but, information is what we need right now. Make sure the new detective gets a fair share of the work. Rosalind's her name, isn't it? Waterloo are going to start bleating soon about lack of progress."

He pulled the first pile of printouts towards him.

As he glanced up, he found Beverly Powell watching him from behind her computer, she smiled and nodded; he had the distinct impression that she gave him a tiny flutter of her eyelashes.

Chapter 16

Terry had his head down, reading reports.

"Anything popped?" Jordan asked.

"A couple of people who are certain that they saw her in town on Saturday and there is CCTV of her in Liverpool One. She had her lunch there, at Nando's. A woman from Kirkby said she saw her at the shops a few times but not lately. Two addresses in such a short time. It's a bit odd. As if she didn't want to be noticed. It's as if she didn't know where to settle, so she was just moving around, adrift somehow. Unless she was hiding but there doesn't seem to be any reason to think that. Anyway, it seems she was there for a while at least."

"Have we received her personnel file yet, from where she worked?"

"Don't think so, boss."

"Chase that up. Maybe it'll give us a clue as to why she moved, an address before that. She came from somewhere even before Kirkby. We need to trace next of kin. They should have sent the file to us by now. When you've done that, go down into town, interview the staff at Nando's. Find out if she met anyone afterwards – whether she seemed upset, worried, all of that stuff. I'll have a quick chat with DC Searle, and then she can go with you. She's not long past her detective's exam and has been marking time in missing persons. She's with us for now. Show her the ropes a bit. Okay?"

"Aye, yeah. No problem."

As he walked away back to his own desk, Jordan looked around the room. Everyone was working hard, but what a team. Cobbled together. Beginners and transfers, officers on loan, a random mix of civilians, and this was potentially one of the biggest cases of his career. For a moment he felt anger, anger at the shortages and the growing loss of experienced officers as they gave up and found work in the private sector. It was followed with a quiver of nerves – he mustn't fail. He squared his shoulders and looked out into the corridor where he saw his new detective looking a bit lost. She was small, pretty, with dark hair pulled back into a pony-tail, and so bloody young. He stepped through the door and held out his hand.

"Okay, Detective Searle? I haven't had a proper chance to say hello."

She blushed. "Yes, sir. Sorry it still feels a bit funny – the detective thing."

"Well congratulations anyway. Terry's on his way out and I want you to go with him. It makes sense, you'll be working closely. I want you to go with him into the city centre. He'll fill you in on the way, and we'll have a chat later. Okay."

"Yes, sir."

That done, Jordan went back to battling to understand the tide tables.

* * *

Within a couple of hours Terry and the new detective were back, by which time Jordan's head was spinning.

"Any luck?" he asked.

"Yeah. She ate on her own at Nando's. A salad and some chicken thighs. The guy behind the counter remembered her when we showed him her picture. They don't have that many people on their own at the weekend and he was a bit miffed because she sat at a table for four. He couldn't say whether she met anyone afterwards, didn't strike him as being upset or worried. But Rosalind here came up with the idea of canvassing the bus drivers. Beatrice would probably have been on the seventeen or the twenty-one. She could have gone on the train, but the bus stop is nearer to her house than the station. So, we checked with the drivers. None of them remembered her. However, most of the buses have CCTV and we've requisitioned all that's available from early afternoon Saturday until later – we've said midnight. She might have stayed in town. It's a start isn't it?"

"Yes, it bloody is. Well done you two. Keep on that will you, get the footage ASAP and we'll make it a priority. At least now we know for certain where she was on Saturday."

Jordan was impressed that Terry was willing to give credit to Rosalind. He hadn't needed to, and it would go a long way to help with the new detective's confidence.

He picked up the papers from his desk and waved them in the air.

"I've been through the tide tables, over and over. I'll be honest, they're too complicated for me – I've managed to speak to a tides expert at the university. He's very knowledgeable and very patient. According to what he's been able to tell me, it would be most likely that, for Beatrice to come ashore at Crosby, her body would need to be thrown into the river, either when the tide was turning, or when it was going out. If she went in earlier then she would have washed the other way. It makes sense, yes?"

"Yes. Seems logical," Terry said.

"So right now, that's between midnight and six in the morning. We need any CCTV from around her house in the mid to late evening. Anywhere. There must be cameras between the bus stop and her road and if your excellent work pans out, DC Searle, we'll be able to find her route. Most important, we'll see if she was with anyone or if anyone was following her. Don't forget she was in her nightclothes when her body was recovered, so she had made it home."

"Unless she stayed with someone else," Terry said.

"Yes, there is always that." Jordan rubbed a hand over his face. "Let's not complicate our thinking with it at the moment. If we see her arriving in Walton, it's a big step forward. None of the house-to-house inquiries have thrown up anything of much interest. Nobody hanging around, no strangers as far as anyone has noticed.

"I am still of the opinion that trying to find where she went in the water will be a real waste of time and I'm leaving that on the back burner for now. I don't reckon we'd ever get the manpower. The bloke at the university was excellent but there are too many possibilities. I hope we don't have to resort to that. Terry, chase up the report from SOCO will you. I should have had that by now. Why does everything take so bloody long?"

"A lot of the route along the river will be covered with cameras though, won't it?" Rosalind asked.

"Yes, of course, but it's the docks at Bootle, the parks and moorings along the bank but plenty of other places aren't covered. We'd probably have to go all the way up to Widnes, maybe even further. My chap was pretty convinced she would have gone in from this side so that narrows it down a small amount at least. I've had one of the civilians contact the people at the Mersey Gateway Bridge, which was a bit obvious and there's nothing there. They checked the full forty-eight hours before she was found. It's well covered with cameras so that at least was relatively easy. There's so much we just don't know yet."

"Right." She nodded. "Oh yes, we called into the printing office to chase up the personnel file. They had it waiting. For some reason they expected us to be picking it up. Anyway, we did."

"Well done."

Terry held out the file.

"More stuff that's unclear I'm afraid. The address they had is the one in Kirkby. They didn't know that she'd moved. She was only temporary, filling in for maternity leave, secretary and filing clerk. She showed them a couple of bills, 'leccy and Sky and the rental agreement and that was enough for them. It's odd, isn't it? But then again, perhaps she just didn't like Kirkby, not a lot of people do. She left the next of kin field blank and nobody followed up on it. I'm following up on her NI number now, but you know how long that can take. I'll keep on at them."

"Hmm. Stick a note on the whiteboard, will you. It is strange. I think we'll go back down there and try to talk to her colleagues. She might have given something away chatting over lunch or making coffee. That's the next job. I'll meet you in the car park in an hour. I'll take my car. Can you two double up?"

Jordan watched them go to find themselves a bite to eat. They seemed to be working effectively together already. Maybe newcomers and borrowed colleagues weren't going to be so much of a handicap after all.

Chapter 17

It was a very small printing firm specialising in wedding stationery and advertising fliers.

"We work on a shoestring," the HR woman told them. She was also the office manager. "Everyone with a computer prints their own stuff these days. That's why we don't use agencies for our temporary staff. They charge a fortune and we find an advert in the Echo usually does the job."

"So that's how she came to you?" Jordan asked.

"Yes, we interviewed her, gave her a typing test, and she started the following week. She was fine, punctual, efficient and pleasant enough. A bit quiet but that's all to the good. People can waste a lot of time gabbing with each other on smoking breaks and what have you."

"So, did she have anyone particularly she talked to, had lunch with?"

"No. I don't think so. We have a staff room and she used to go in there. I sat with her a couple of times, but as I say she was quiet."

"Is there anything at all that you can tell us? Did she mention a family, friends – maybe even where she came from?"

"No, but she did have an accent. Not that strong but enough to notice."

"Right. And?" Jordan said.

"Newcastle type, that way I would think, very northern. The way she said certain words, you know. Like that bloke that used to be in the builder's programme – in Germany a while back? That's it. *Auf Wiedersehen, Pet.*"

Jordan shook his head.

"No, ha, probably before your time. They always say you're getting old when policemen start to look young and you and your two officers look as though you've just left school. No offence meant."

"Ha, none taken. I feel ancient myself just looking at some of my colleagues these days. We'll try not to take up too much time. But we really need to find out more about Beatrice. If you think of anything that might help, please do let us know."

Jordan handed her his card and scribbled his mobile number on the back.

Circles within circles, it was frustrating, but they had a tiny bit more.

* * *

Back in the office Jordan put in a request to try and have the appeal widened.

"The national news would be brilliant, sir," he said to Richard Cross. "If she's from Northumberland we need to go nationwide."

"I'll see what I can do. We can push it on the internet, get our friends in Northumberland to do a couple of posts, mention the possible origins at least. It'll be on HOLMES already. This is floundering a bit, Detective Inspector. I had hoped for more by now. I'm seeing Campbell later and I know he's going to be chewing my ears off."

"We're doing what we can, sir. Now we have her name and where she was in the hours before she died, I feel that we are moving along."

"Aye well, move along faster, if you would." And he hung up the phone.

"Have you got a minute?"

Jordan looked up to find Vivienne Bailey, the Scene of Crimes Sergeant, at his desk. He was aware of Terry sidling up to join them.

"Of course. I hope you've got something interesting for me," Jordan said.

"I have a report of sorts, nothing terribly conclusive or surprising I'm afraid." She dragged a chair towards her. "We've finished with our examination of the house. We've been through it very thoroughly."

"I don't doubt it," Jordan said. "Erm, would you like coffee? We have instant."

"Okay, go on then."

Before he could move Terry had leapt up and crossed to the small table by the window. Jordan smiled to himself.

Sergeant Bailey placed a file folder on the desk.

"This is all in a report emailed to you, but I reckoned you'd have some questions, so I came up. Thought it would save time."

"Okay. I'm grateful. I haven't had a chance to look at that yet."

"Well, we went right through. Every room, and it was well looked after."

"Yeah it looked pretty tidy from what I saw."

She nodded her head.

"The kitchen was cleaner than a whistle. Sink had been cleaned and the drains had been flushed with bleach so nothing nice and juicy in the U-bend. Interestingly the cupboard under the sink, you know, where everyone keeps their cleaning things?"

Jordan nodded.

"That was almost empty. Dusters and brushes but no bottles of cleaning stuff. I reckon whoever did the clean-up took them with them. Hard to clean prints off bottles and sprays, it's the shape of the handles, quicker to remove them and dump them off-site. Bloody television programmes tell everyone our little tricks. Should be banned. No fingerprints apart from your victim in the places you would imagine. There were a couple of tissues in the bathroom bin, but they had lipstick on that matched a partly used one from the bedroom. Apart from that it was very clean."

She shrugged and reached up to take the mug from Terry.

"So, you didn't get anything?" Jordan said.

She grinned at him.

"Don't be daft, we always get something. You can scrub till the cows come home but humans leave traces, we can't help it – skin flakes, hair, snot, saliva. I just wanted to make the point that whoever lived there kept a nice home. Credit where it's due and I thought it might be relevant at some stage. I've put the blood type, et cetera, in the email. I won't bother you with it now. We've sent off for DNA but that'll take a while and to be honest if it's not the victim's, I'll be a dutchman."

"So, what did you get?"

As entertaining and easy on the eye as she was, Jordan was becoming impatient.

"Blood, in the kitchen, on the floor tiles, in the grout really. When we got the black light on it, there was in fact evidence of quite a lot of it. A few spots and splashes on the front of the cupboard, which had been wiped, but it was in the woodgrain. Low down all of it, and some under the tabletop. They missed that, whoever did the clean-up job. So, I would say she was on the floor when she was struck. There was splash, possibly from the weapon, which must have been pretty gory, and there was one tiny piece of 'matter' stuck to the underside of the table."

"Matter?" Jordan said.

"Yeah, brain I should think. We've sent it to the lab, but I bet you it'll be grey brain matter. Pictures are in the file. This coffee's horrible, it's got sugar in." She slapped the mug onto Jordan's desk and gave him a wave as she walked away. "See ya." She left the door to slam behind her.

Terry gazed after her.

"Put your tongue away, Detective Constable, we've got a report to read, and anyway she didn't like your coffee."

Chapter 18

It was only putting off the inevitable, but Graham had been rejecting calls all afternoon. He knew who they were from and he just couldn't handle it. It had won him some funny looks from his secretary and the blokes in the office outside. He cursed the open-door policy, the first name basis that they all worked under.

"Avoiding the missus?" Tony had said and they had all laughed. "Her hormones playing up, eh. Just you wait, you haven't seen nothing yet. My missus was like a bloody nutcase at times."

Graham had to laugh along with them.

"Nah, it's sales calls. I might have to change my number. Don't know how they've got hold of this one."

In the toilets he called Rose.

"I'll be late, love. Got some urgent stuff to do. Don't wait for me. Have your dinner."

Later, he watched the room empty, listened to the banter and afterwards sat in the silence. He walked around the floor, checked in the toilets, men's and women's and in the snack room. Everyone had gone. The next time his phone rang, the screen showing 'withheld number', he was at his desk. He closed his eyes just for a moment, took a breath.

"What?"

"Oh, at last. I was going to pop round to your house. Thought maybe your phone was out of order."

"Don't. Don't you ever do that. I swear if you do that, I'll…"

"Yeah, you'll what? Listen, mate, you need to get your head into gear. I want that money. I need it by Sunday at the latest. I'll ring you again on Saturday and give you instructions. Don't play silly buggers any more or I'll have no choice but to have a word with your wife, maybe tell her a couple of your little secrets. You don't want that. I know you don't. After all, that was what started this, wasn't it? You and your secrets."

"I'll have it for you. But this is it. Don't think you can blackmail me. This is the only money I'll be able to get and even this is going to be incredibly hard. Don't come back for more."

"I'm so pleased that you are working 'incredibly hard' for me, I really am. Tell me, when it all happened, way back when. What did you think? Did you think you'd got away with it all scot free? I bet you did. I bet all these years you've been telling yourself you'd dodged the bullet with this one. Just goes to show, doesn't it? You really never leave anything behind. Anyway, don't worry I won't be back. I need to get away for a while and then I'm done with you. I don't need your sort in my life, you filthy bastard. You really are the lowest of the low. Wait for my call."

That was it, he was gone. Graham turned to his machine. All day he had been mulling over how he was going to do this and now, he thought he had it all sorted. He would go to the older investments, the settled ones. The ones that nobody really thought about much anymore. There were some that had been ticking over for years, up and down a bit with the stock market but low-risk and unexciting. The main thing was that they weren't often drawn down on. People were told up front: this is long term, for your retirement. The longer you leave them alone the better it will be. In truth how many people checked up on them – they just trusted the company to look after them. Not like the new customers, checking every day some of them, but once people had confidence they stopped worrying.

So, he would skim a bit off the top of a few of them, finagle the figures and slide the money into another account. By the time it was noticed, when the annual reports were due out, he would have put it back. He might have to go and borrow some of the money for that, and it was going to cost him but there was no other way.

It was okay, it was all short-term and in a couple of months he'd be free and clear. Okay, the interest from the loan company would be crippling but he'd work hard, he'd make sure his bonus was massive, like it was in the early days and he'd sort it then.

That bloke had scared him though. With the comment about going to his house. Did he really know where he lived? Yes, of course he did, he'd sent that letter. He felt cold sweat trickle down between his shoulder blades. If it all came out his whole world would come crashing down. The bloke was right, he had thought he'd dodged the bullet. How could he have possibly known about the girl's existence?

He got his head down and began to work, it wasn't that difficult, not like stealing really. Just clicking buttons, shifting totals.

His fingers hovered over the enter key. He had been able to collect together most of the money. All he needed to do now was to send it to his account. He gulped, rubbed his hands together, they were sticky with sweat. This was a tipping point. If ever he was found out he would lose his licence, his job for certain, his reputation – everything. It was true that he had sailed close to the wind in some of his dealings. It was what they did, not exactly illegal but playing the game, saving money for the clients with knowledge and skill. He was good at it, he enjoyed it. Now, because of one stupid mistake, way back in the past, he was being forced to risk everything to pay off some creep who had found out by accident things that Graham had truly believed were ancient history.

He stood from the desk, walked back and forth. It was late now, nearly ten o'clock. He needed a drink. He sat back in his chair. He wagged the mouse to wake the screen. Just one more action.

He couldn't do it. It wasn't that he was a wimp, it was just that he wasn't really a criminal. He had made mistakes, everyone made mistakes, especially when they were young and hot-blooded, but this was too far. He could go to jail for this.

He put it back, all of it, covered his tracks as best he could. If someone looked closely enough there was evidence, but he handled these accounts and he would make sure there was no reason for anyone to look.

He knew what he had to do. By the time he logged out and turned off the lights he had transferred the house savings into a new account. Rose would be devastated but there was no other way. The money would be in his account in the morning. His mouth was dry, and his heart pounded, but at least he wasn't a thief.

Chapter 19

Beverly Powell was waiting for Jordan when he arrived at work. He was becoming used to the woman being first in, last out. She took her lunch at her desk, a sandwich and coffee from a small flask. She was keen, he had to give her that.

"Hi, how are you?"

"I'm fine, sir. Thank you. I almost rang you about this." She waved a paper in the air. "It's a promising ID after the alert up in Northumberland. Someone who thinks they recognise our victim."

"Excellent."

"It's a carer, in a hospice up there. She seems pretty sure that she knows the woman but knew her as Betty, erm…" Beverly turned the paper around to peer at it. "Yes, here it is, Betty Sharp. Apparently, her mother is a patient. Very ill. You know, really ill. Not going to get better. Anyway, she says that this 'Betty' used to visit every day until a couple of months ago. Her mother went into a coma and the daughter said that she had to go away. She left but telephoned every day until just a few days ago. They tried to contact her because the mother is deteriorating but couldn't reach her."

Jordan took the sheet of paper and read through the notes.

"So, her mother is out of it, we can't talk to her. That's a shame." He pursed his lips. "Beverly, get in touch with DC Denn for me. It's seven-thirty now – ask him to get in as soon as he can and be ready. We're going up there. I want to see where she came from. It might be quicker to go by rail, so–"

"The train takes over three hours, sir. It's quicker by road if there are no hold-ups and at the moment there are only a couple of small sections of roadworks on the M6."

"Right. How come you know all this?" He smiled at her. "Have you got relatives up there?"

"No, sir. When I read the report, I thought you might want to go and just did the research. If you did want to use the train, they go from Lime Street about once an hour about ten minutes to."

"That's impressive work. Thank you."

"No problem, sir. I'll get on to DC Denn. The report from Sergeant Bailey has come through, it's fairly extensive. Do you want me to go through it and pick out anything that's relevant?"

Jordan looked up at her. He paused, choosing his words carefully.

"I think it might be better if you just leave that with me. I need to go through it all myself. Just to make sure I'm completely aware, you know. But, in the meantime would you make sure DC Searle has a copy, she can have a read while we're away. I'll call her later."

He saw the change. Moments before, the woman had been smiling, slightly flushed, her eyes sparkling at him. Now she lifted her chin, stiffened her shoulders and tossed her hair.

"Fine. It should be in your inbox. I'll go and make that phone call."

Jordan watched her go, aware that he had offended her. He sighed and reached for the phone.

He rang home.

"Hello, love. I have to go to Newcastle, so I don't know when I'll be back. It'll probably be late."

"Oh. Okay."

"Is there something wrong?"

"No, it's fine. It's just that I've had a letter saying I've got the job. The one at the Citizens Advice. I was hoping we could celebrate. I was going to book a table at the pub. But it's okay. We'll do it some other time."

"Sorry, love. This really can't be avoided."

"No, no it's okay. I'll call Lizzie, see if she can come over. Derek can mind the kids. Take care, Jordan."

He felt bad. She had sounded very disappointed. She was always supportive, always understanding, but he knew very well that, for the marriage to work, it needed constant attention and he would have to make this up to her. It would need to be afterwards though. Right now, he must focus.

Chapter 20

The sound of Rose in the bathroom woke Graham. He tried squirming under the duvet and dragging the pillow over his head, but it was no good. He hated listening to her retching, and he had no choice but to push himself into a sitting position on the side of the bed.

"Are you alright, love?"

There was a groan and a couple of words which were lost in the noise of the flush. He slid his feet into slippers and went to put the kettle on. He really had hoped to avoid her today. She had been in bed when he arrived home last night and didn't stir while he sat on the settee drinking whisky. The alcohol had come home to wreak revenge this morning. He had a pounding head and a mouth that felt like the proverbial bottom of a parrot cage. He went into the downstairs loo for a pee then a couple of glasses of cold water in the kitchen.

By the time he'd put the coffee on, for him, the tea, for her, Rose was trailing along the hallway, a bit pale but smiling.

"I'll be glad when this bit is over. Mind you, Mary at work said that she was sick the whole nine months with both of hers."

"Yuk."

She came up behind him and wrapped her arms around his waist. He could feel the swell of her belly when she was this close. Guilt swamped him for a minute, and he had to move away. He took hold of her hand.

"You sit here, love. I'll get your tea and a piece of toast, yeah?"

"Lovely. I missed you last night. I waited up but you were very late."

"I know, sorry. I had to sort out some old accounts."

If he stuck as close as possible to the truth, then the chance of a making a mistake was lessened. He knew this from the past.

"I wanted to show you something," Rose said. She leaned over to a shelf of jugs and bowls and pulled an A4 envelope from the top. "I got these yesterday. I thought we could go tomorrow and have a look. I can ring and make the appointment during lunch today."

She pulled out several glossy brochures all headed with the logo of a local estate agent. So, it was to come this soon. The reckoning.

He dragged the second chair away from the table and sat down opposite to his wife. She was wagging one of the leaflets in the air.

"This one's lovely. A bit far out of town but there's bus routes and a station not far away and the main thing is there are great schools."

He took the paper from her hand and laid it on the table and then wrapped his fingers around hers.

"Listen, love. There's something we need to talk about."

She tipped her head to one side. "Let me just get my tea."

"Oh right, yeah sorry. Here, let me."

Once the drinks were in front of them, he started again.

"Okay, I don't know quite how to say this, and I know you're going to be disappointed and I'm really sorry. But the thing is – well – it looks as though, for now, just for the time being anyway we might have to shelve the house move."

She froze with the cup halfway to her lips, lowered it slowly back to the tabletop.

"What?"

"Just for the time being. I've been doing the figures and, right now, it's not going to be possible for us to move. We'll have to stay here."

She looked around as if she had never seen their home before.

"Stay here? In this place? Here?"

"Yes. It'll be okay. We'll have the second bedroom decorated. Come on it's a nice house and the garden's big enough for one little baby. It'll be just for a bit. Until I get the money sorted out."

"How do you mean? The money's sorted. We've been saving for ages. We've been planning for ages. It's all organised. Okay, there was that few thousand for the car, I know that was a pain but by the time we're ready to move we'll have made that back; you said the investments have been doing well."

"I know, I know, but I've had some other expenses, unexpected things have come up and right now is not the best time to be doing this. I'm really sorry, love – I really am."

She began to shake her head.

"No, no, no. This is not happening. I'm sorry, Graham, but we are moving. I'm not having our baby here. I'm not bringing our child home to this place. A teeny garden, a busy road outside. Think of the pollution from car exhausts, we've already agreed this. What about schools, no child of mine is going to that comprehensive. Oh no. Anyway, what are these expenses? What can you possibly have been spending money on that I don't know about? Christ, have you become some sort of gambler or something?"

Her fists were clenched on the tabletop and tears had sprung to her eyes.

"Don't get upset, love. It's years until we have to worry about school. There's plenty of time for that," he said.

"Don't get upset. You are kidding me, right? Look at the soddin' time. I have to go – I've got a meeting this morning. But this is not over, Graham. This is not over at all. We're moving, before this baby arrives, we are moving. You promised me, and no lies about extra expenses and shortage of money are going to get you off the hook. I can't believe you've done this. I'm a wreck now and I've got to go into work. You bastard. This is not finished, not by a long chalk."

She stamped from the room, thundered upstairs and he heard her slamming about in the bedroom before the sound of the door and the roar of her car from outside. He lowered his head onto his hands and sighed.

'That went well,' he muttered.

Chapter 21

Jordan met Terry Denn in the car park.

"Will you drive for the first leg? I can have a look at the report on the computer and I need to send a couple of emails."

Once they were on their way he logged on to his tablet. Jordan pinged an email to Vivienne Bailey asking if she'd chased the DNA results. He received a snotty response very quickly suggesting that if he was so keen to tell her how to do her job, he could handle the next putrefied corpse they came across.

"You'd better watch your step there, boss, or you might be the next corpse," Terry said.

"We didn't find Beatrice's computer. She must have had one, surely. Unless she's been using the PC in her office. We requisitioned that, didn't we?"

"Yeah, they have it, but I reckon the techies haven't looked at it yet. They are snowed under and we didn't think it was urgent, to be honest. The woman from the printers was adamant that they didn't allow employees to do personal work on the office equipment. It's a bit tight-arsed but they seem like an old-fashioned firm. She has been on the phone a couple of times complaining. They need it back. They can lay down rules as much as they like but I bet people don't really stick to them. I mean you can browse incognito, can't you? It doesn't take a lot of skill to hide what you've been doing from a cursory search."

"Okay, I'll make some calls and see if we can push it through. Bit disappointing though. I can't believe she didn't have one of her own. Not in this day and age. We haven't got her phone either. Mind, I'm not surprised. There must have been one because there was no landline in the house, but they are the first thing that people get rid of these days. The number the nursing home was using was the same one that she gave to her work, so I reckon it's been ditched. She would have wanted the home to be able to contact her, wouldn't she? So, she would have kept it charged up and switched on."

"Let's hope this Newcastle lead leads somewhere anyway. Up to now we haven't even got a motive for this killing."

"It could just be random, couldn't it?" Terry said.

"Yes, of course. I hate that idea, but yes it could. Though all indications are that she was taken from her home – that's odd if it was just a chance encounter. When we find out why she moved, left her mother at what sounds to have been a critical time, and started up a whole new life, miles away, then that's got to help. It doesn't fit with what we've heard about her. She was a caring daughter, so what happened? They are still going through the CCTV from the city centre and the buses. Nothing yet."

* * *

The nursing home was a modern building set within a small, landscaped garden. There were flowers in the entrance hall and the place was clean and warm. The carer who had contacted them met them in reception and showed them through to a small visitor's room.

"I'm in a bit of trouble. The manager is proper fashed because I didn't go through her. But to be honest, when I saw Betty, her picture and your request for information, I was so shocked, I just phoned. Anyway, Mrs Brett, that's the manager, is goin' on about data protection, privacy and all that palaver. She wants to talk to you."

"I'll have a word with her. Most of the rules about data protection cease to apply when there's been a suspicious death," Jordan told her.

"Thanks so much." The girl's eyes flooded with tears and for a moment Jordan wasn't sure whether it was relief or grief until she spoke again.

"She was a lovely lassie, Betty. She came in every day and sat with her mum. Good days, and bad days – didn't make any difference. She came straight from work and had a cup of tea and a cake. Weekends she would come in from shopping down the town, show her mum what she'd bought."

"Is this definitely her?"

Jordan took out the image they had. The girl glanced at the picture and nodded.

"Is it true that she was killed?"

"Unfortunately, yes. But you've really helped. Coming forward like this will help us to find out what happened to her, thank you," Jordan said.

"Is there any way we can speak to her mother?" Terry asked.

"No, there's no point, she's non-communicative. Poor lamb. She's been with us a few months and she wasn't like this at first but now she is at the end of life really. She's got a brain tumour and it's metastasised, there's not much time left. That's why we wanted to contact Betty – am I supposed to call her Beatrice, now then? Mind you, maybe it's for the best, Vera not knowing about this. They were so close."

"There was no husband, no other relatives?" Jordan asked.

The girl shook her head. "Never anyone we knew about."

"And you don't know where Beatrice worked, while she lived here?" Terry was making notes in his book as they talked.

"No, they were very private, and we didn't need to know that, as long as we had the contact details and a home address."

"There was no answer to your phone calls recently?"

"No, it was just dead. We thought at first maybe it was out of charge or something like that. It wasn't though, was it?"

She dabbed at her eyes and then stood up.

"I'll get you the address."

"Thank you so much, miss…" Jordan said.

"Ach, just call me Tracy."

"Thank you again, Tracy. You've been a great help. Take my card and if you think of anything else, anything at all, even if you don't think it's important, please just call myself or DC Denn, would you?"

When she came back with the piece of paper, the address written neatly along with names and phone numbers, Tracy looked up at Jordan, pursed her lips for a moment and then made a decision.

"Look, I know this is just me, I have no real proof or anything but there was one day, when Betty was visiting. Not long ago, but when Vera began to go downhill, and not long before her daughter stopped coming. I took them a cup of tea and there was a terrible atmosphere. Vera was crying and Betty was standing by the window. She looked awful, tense and upset. I asked if everything was okay and they didn't really answer. I put it down to the situation, it's hard watching someone fade away, but it wasn't normally like that, after all that's what this place is about. Usually they were quite cheerful, in spite of everything. Anyway, you said, if I thought of anything – to tell you. I don't know that it can help but it bothered me, a lot."

Chapter 22

The house was a small terrace with a tiny, paved space in the front. A couple of pots with dead plants in stood under the windows to one side of the front door. They knocked, though it was obvious that the place was empty. No-one had swept the path for a while. It was littered with paper and plastic food containers. The windows were dirty, the curtains part closed and when Terry peered through the window, his hands on either side of his face to cut out glare, there was no sign of life in the little living room.

Jordan rang Bev.

"I need a warrant to enter a house in Newcastle." He gave her an address. "I really don't want to have to come back up here, so see if it can be expedited, will you?"

"Leave it with me, sir. I'll get on it straight away."

They knocked at the houses on either side but there was no answer. A young woman pushing a baby buggy up the street stopped. All she could tell them was that the woman who lived there had been taken ill and was away somewhere and she hadn't seen the daughter 'for ages'.

It was nothing they didn't know already. As she walked away the girl turned back to them.

"You could have a word with me granny. She's in the house now and she's lived here all her life. There's nothing she doesn't know about the road. Number seventeen, that way." She waved a hand behind her. "She'll be happy to have a bit of craic. She's real nebby, can't mind her own business."

With a laugh the girl walked on.

They had nothing to lose and so with a cup of tea and a fruit scone in front of them, in a tidy overwarm living room, they had a word with Barbara Price.

"Babs to me friends."

"So, do you know the women at number twenty-five?" Jordan said.

"Not know them, know them. They weren't from round here. Newcomers."

"How long have they lived there?"

"Oh, only about twenty years or so."

"That's newcomers?" Terry shook his head.

"Aye, it is to me. I've been here all me life. That's more than eighty years now. Born and bred in this house and it were me dad's before me."

"Wow. You must know everything that's gone on then," Jordan said.

"I'm not nebby, if that's what you mean."

Jordan bit back a smile at the contradiction of the younger woman's opinion.

"No, I'm sure you're not. Still though, you remember them coming to live here?"

"Aye, I do. Vera had a bit of a time being as she was, you know…" Babs leaned forward and whispered, "Unmarried and her with a babby."

She nodded as she leaned back.

"Oh, I know now it's nothing. Everybody does it, but back then it were still something to be frowned upon. Mind you it were a bonny little bairn and after a while nobody bothered anymore."

Jordan showed her the picture.

"Aye, that's Betty. They never really got that friendly though. Always a bit standoffish, kept themselves close. Mind, she went out to work, Vera, down the school lately. I don't know where before that, a café in the town when Betty were wee. A couple of shops and then later at the school, I think that was so she could keep an eye on her bairn. She were always whatchamacallit, possessive – aye that's it, possessive."

"Was she a teacher?" Terry asked.

"No, no, bonny lad. She were a dinner lady. Once that Betty grew up and got herself work, Vera just worked in the charity shop. Sorting out the clothes and such. A bit of a nothing job but I suppose it filled her day. It's shut down now, but anyway she were taken bad and couldn't do nothing after that. I think she's in a home or something now and I haven't seen that girl for weeks. Perhaps she's staying with her. They do that, don't they? She must be proper bad." The old woman shook her head. "Not that old either. Poor thing."

It wasn't a lot of help, although now they had more confirmation that they were looking in the right place.

Chapter 23

They found a café, steamy and smelling of hot fat and stewed coffee. Terry bought a cheese and bacon beefburger, Jordan ordered a smaller version without the cheese or bacon, they shared a plate of chips.

Halfway through the meal a message, with a copy of the warrant allowing them entry to the house pinged into Jordan's phone.

Beverly had attached a comment.

It's owned by Vera Sharp. We have been looking her up on the system. Nothing as yet. I have searched for birth records in Newcastle without success but there is one in Liverpool which looks promising. Following it through. Nothing for Beatrice Sharp either.

n.b. The NI number she had given the printing company was incorrect – fake? They have just been in touch to let us know. Seems she hadn't been with them long enough for it to be highlighted. Now it has. Will keep you informed.

"Okay, finish those chips, Terry," Jordan said. "We can get into the house and with luck now, we'll get more information. Interesting that it could be the family originated in Liverpool."

They didn't want to break in, and they didn't really want to wait for a locksmith.

"Maybe a neighbour has a key," Terry said.

"If they're not in though, be quicker to get a locksmith. Oh, hang on." Jordan pulled out his phone and scrolled through the recent calls. "The nursing home," he said.

A quick conversation and a short wait and they knew there was a house key in the possessions of Vera Sharp.

* * *

The house smelled damp and closed-up. However, when they walked into the kitchen, they found that the fridge had been emptied, unplugged and left open. There was no waste food in the bins or cupboards and the dishes were washed and stacked neatly on shelves. There was a dishcloth folded on the draining board. In the back yard were a couple more pots, the plants in them struggling against neglect.

"It's been locked up for a while, hasn't it?" Terry said. "But she didn't just leave on the spur of the moment."

Upstairs there were three bedrooms, one had been turned into a workroom. There was a sewing machine, a few storage boxes filled with fabric and sewing supplies and a desk set under the window. A lead with three extension sockets was coiled on the floor underneath and in the drawer, they found a computer mouse and a pair of earphones.

"I guess this was her computer set-up. So, no desktop machine. It certainly looks as though she intended to be gone for a while. It proves she had a computer though."

The larger of the two bedrooms had been the older woman's. It was obvious from the style of clothes still hanging in the wardrobe. Not old lady things but certainly not for a young woman. In the other bedroom they found a couple of pairs of old jeans and some worn tops and washed-out nightwear.

Downstairs the tiny front room was furnished with a settee and two matching armchairs, the television, and a sound system, run of the mill and inexpensive. There was a table in the window with an empty vase and a small ornament of a mother and baby. It was all rather sad. Jordan went into the dining room and began rooting in the sideboard cupboards. One held china and glasses but the other was empty. The shelves were dusty and screwed in the back corner was a single piece of paper. Jordan smoothed it out onto the tabletop. It was a page from a diary planner. There were a couple of doctor and hospital appointments written neatly in the spaces.

"The place has been de-personalised," he said.

"How do you mean?"

"There are no photographs, no family papers of any kind. No school reports or swimming certificates, all that stuff. My mum has boxes of it. I think she's kept just about every document there ever was for all of us. We know that the two of them have lived here all through Beatrice's childhood, so where are the souvenirs?"

"Yeah. My mum has some, not as much as that, but important stuff. Birth certificates and what have you. Nobody ever looks at them, but she's got them stowed away in the spare room."

Jordan walked through to the kitchen and peered out of the grimy window. The key hung on a hook beside the door and he allowed himself a tut at the security risk. Out in the yard there was a washing line sagging across the space, a couple of abandoned pegs flicked back and forth in the chilly breeze. In the sheltered corner where the two walls met, furthest from the house, there was a small metal bin. He removed the lid.

"Terry, look at this."

There was a pile of ash, layers of it and as the breeze hit the inside of the container it puffed upwards to float out and gently fall onto the damp ground. Jordan flicked at the front of his jacket.

"Bugger it." He dragged a pair of nitrile gloves from his jeans pocket and reached down into the debris. "It's all here, look." He held up the corner of a photograph, just one tiny piece.

The edges were singed and all that was discernible was the vague image of some trees against the sky. He picked up another scrap.

"This looks like a certificate of some sort. It's probably going to be a complete waste of time, but we need a forensic team to go through this. There might be something of use. When you have piles of paper it's surprising how the stuff in the middle can survive. I'm not holding out much hope though. This looks pretty well burned. I'll send a message to Beverly to arrange to have the place examined but I reckon we should just head off back. We're not going to find much here; she didn't intend anyone to. I wonder what it was that made her want to obliterate all traces of what would seem to have been a happy life. I reckon that what was left of her will now be back in Liverpool. She had finished with this."

Chapter 24

Graham had a bitch of a day. Between the whisky hangover and the row with Rose he was already in a bad place when he arrived at the office. He logged on, paranoid now about what he had almost done the day before. He went over all the old accounts repeatedly, looking for the error, looking for the tell-tale hiccup in the figures that would expose him. He couldn't find anything, but he was drawn back to it over and over. The panic and the despair he felt for letting Rose down was ghastly. But it was nothing compared to the guilt about the girl.

It pestered at him constantly, always there in the back of his mind. She was dead. Okay he didn't know her. He'd never met her and until recently he didn't even know she existed. Now she was dead. It didn't matter how he spun it, she was dead because of him. It was true that he had never laid a finger on her but if it hadn't been for him, there would be no reason for her to be lying in a morgue. No reason for her to have been tossed in the river before that. If he'd had more backbone, if he'd told that bloke to sod off, she would still be alive. The thought overwhelmed him at times and he felt the tears start, his breathing quickened, his heart pounded and through it all he had to sit at his desk, review columns of figures, make phone calls to strangers and not let his guard down, not for a moment.

He tried to imagine his life a year from now. The new baby, his promotion, maybe a new house, though that seemed unlikely. Rose happy and fulfilled, and all these problems just a horrible nightmare. He had to hang on to that – he had to get through this.

When the bloke rang him again, he'd do exactly as he was told. He'd pay him and then he'd put this behind him. Then there was that other problem, like a malignant spot in his mind, growing and growing no matter how hard he tried to push it away. Beatrice, the news reports called her. This Beatrice, though she was a stranger, she was not unconnected. Though they had no shared history, she was part of his back story, intricately woven into the very fabric of his life.

It would drive him mad. It was constant, like a dripping tap, whenever he tried to empty his mind it was there – the knowledge of just what a terrible, unforgiveable thing he had done.

* * *

He dragged himself through the day, couldn't eat, snapped at junior colleagues, and was impatient and ill-tempered with clients. This was going to destroy him. More than the other option would have done, more than the thing that he had thought could be the worst possible.

Exposure.

This guilt would finish him. He had to end it, completely and utterly. There could be no loose threads. He couldn't go through the rest of his life wondering if he'd get a phone call, a letter or a knock on the door.

One option was to take his own life – he googled ideas about suicide. It was shocking and sickening. He imagined Rose, with their baby, on her own and maybe even finding out the truth after all. That wasn't the solution. He had to finish this somehow. But he didn't know how.

He arrived home late, haggard and exhausted and she was waiting for him, as he had known she would be. Furious and tearful. She stood before him her arms folded across her chest. Anger sparked in her eyes.

"Before we do anything else, we are going to sort this out. I want to know just what the hell you've been doing. I've looked at the accounts. You say you've had expenses. What expenses? Just what is going on with you, Graham? Where is the rest of our money? Half of that is mine. What have you done with my money?"

He put down his briefcase, dragged off his jacket and went to the sideboard to pour a glass of gin. He downed it in one, no ice, no mixer – just liquid courage.

"Sit down, Rose. Just sit down please and I'll tell you. I've been struggling with this all day. I feel awful, I didn't want to tell you any of this but now I see that it's the only way. Afterwards, when I've told you, you can do whatever you think is best. I'll agree to anything – I'm exhausted with it. I can't find a way out of it, so, whatever you decide, I'll agree to. Sit down, love, and just let me say this."

Chapter 25

Jordan and Terry drove back down the M6 with the end-of-day traffic. It was grey and drizzling and the inside of their car felt damp and stuffy despite the heating. They were disappointed and dispirited. Terry swigged from a can of fizzy drink and scattered crisp crumbs on the seats and carpets. Jordan bit his tongue at the mess. The empty packet was thrown into the footwell and to avoid making a comment that would show him to be uptight, he ran through the day's events.

"All we've done really," he said, "is confirmed the name of the victim and that she'd changed it, slightly. We've seen what was probably the home she had lived in before moving to Liverpool, and very little else."

A forensic team had moved in just before they left with evidence bags and labels and cameras but, apart from the small chance of finding something useful in the middle of the mess in the metal bin in the garden, they couldn't think of anything positive to say about the day.

"The DCI is going to be a bit antsy about the cost of this trip and the SOCO team and what have you. To be honest I don't expect to find that much but we might get to understand her better. I'm wracking my brain and I can't really come up with much to tell him," Jordan said.

"We know she wasn't married. We know that there doesn't seem to be anyone who would be looking for her. I guess that's something. We know for certain that she used to live there, and seems to have left for good," Terry muttered.

"Yeah, but we don't have any real idea why. We certainly don't have any better idea of why she was killed. There was nothing in the house to give us a clue about that, and the couple of people who knew her didn't give us much, did they?"

"It doesn't look as though she had changed her name legally. She was just using a different one and it wasn't that much of a change. That's a bit odd. I mean if she was really running from her past in some way you would expect her to do it all officially," Terry said.

"But you do have to refer to your previous name and give reasons. Doing it this way it wouldn't need any explanation, I suppose. She seems to have been a loving daughter, she and her mother were close so why leave her now, at the end of her life and cut off all ties?"

"But, she hadn't, not really, she was still phoning the nursing home, wasn't she?"

"True. But I wonder what happened to make her want to leave at this point," Jordan said.

"There was the comment by the nurse. The day she said they were both upset."

"Yeah, but you would be, wouldn't you? They both knew time was running out. It's terrible and stressful. Of course, they were upset."

"Yeah, I suppose," Terry answered.

The phone was connected to the Bluetooth so they both heard the message when Beverly Powell rang. They picked up the slightly breathless note in her voice and glanced at each other.

"Sir, we've had some luck with the CCTV from a bus. We've found our victim. She made her way home from the city centre in the early evening. The bus was quite busy, and she sat on the upper deck. She didn't have much with her, just a small bag, looked like food. She alighted at the stop nearest to her home."

Terry screwed up his nose and raised his eyebrows.

"So, nothing unusual then?" he asked.

"It seems there is something, DC Searle thinks it might be important. She's viewing it again but thought you'd want to know. I thought I'd bring you up to date."

"Okay. And…" Terry sounded impatient.

"There is a white van which appears to follow the bus, even when it stops it doesn't overtake."

Terry shook his head and held up his hands palm upwards in a 'so what' gesture.

"They might just have been avoiding overtaking a passenger vehicle, exercising careful road sense," Jordan said.

"Yes, sir, but after the victim alighted, the van drove past a short way, turned and went back the way the bus had come. Then it parked in one of the narrow roads in Walton. Later the driver is seen walking past the shops. He went into one of the pubs and stayed there until closing time, picked up the van and drove into the victim's road. He can be seen leaving again some time later. Everyone is viewing more footage now to see if we can spot him. He went along Queens Drive towards Balliol Road but there are roadworks along there and the cameras are out. But he could have been heading towards the docks. DC Searle wondered if we should requisition footage from any private cameras along that route."

"Have you not got the registration?"

"It was partly obscured, sir. That was another thing that alerted us, well the detective constable really. It could have been dirt, the vehicle was in need of cleaning, but DC Searle thought it might be deliberate to avoid recognition.

We're trying to trace vans of the same age and make with a registration, to match the partial that was visible."

"Okay. Who spotted him?"

Beverly paused, eventually she muttered, "DC Searle, sir."

"Excellent. Keep me informed. Tell everyone, good work. We'll be back in a couple of hours. Tell DC Searle I'd like her to stay."

"Just the DC, sir?"

"I think so, she can update me. No point in everyone working overtime."

Beverly didn't bother to say goodbye.

"I'm impressed with Searle," Jordan said.

"Yeah, me too," Terry said with a grin.

His own phone rang which saved him from the cutting comment Jordan had been about to make. Listening to one side of the conversation, Jordan nonetheless picked up on the urgency and noted Terry sliding more upright in the seat, his shoulders tensing.

He clicked off the phone and put it back into his pocket.

"Problem?" Jordan asked.

"Me mam. She's been mugged. Had her pension nicked and her bag with her phone. Can you drop me off at home, boss?"

"Of course. Do you want to get on to the station, have someone go round, or is there someone already there?"

"No, no. That was my cousin. He's with her. She's not hurt too bad, just a bit shaken up and she's mad, very mad."

"But you need to get someone round there, to take a statement and what have you."

"No, it's fine. If you just drop me off at home, we'll deal with it."

"How do you mean?"

"Really, boss, it's fine. Just leave it with me. She wouldn't want the fuss, wouldn't want strangers in the house. Not while she's upset."

"Okay. If that's what you want."

"Yep. That's what I want."

Chapter 26

Ben hadn't had the chance to sort a new car, and probably wouldn't be able to for a while, the way things had turned out. He would just have to use the van. He could hire a car but why bother, it'd mean filling in paperwork. He didn't intend to use a taxi to the airport and none of his mates could be relied on to keep their mouths shut if the shit really hit the fan. He had to do this on his own as much as possible.

He went down to the lock-up and removed the number plates. They were easy to cut up with the tin snips and he put the pieces in various different bins in the area. A quick call to Jerry, who ran a car repair shop, sorted out a replacement set of plates. Jerry had no idea what his registration number was and just did as he was told. A couple of numbers transposed, that's all it needed, that and some dirt and dust smeared around. It would work okay as long as he didn't get into any sort of a situation. He only needed it for a day or two and then he'd be away. He'd leave it up near the airport. It'd be ages before anyone bothered about it.

Once his mother had gone to the bingo he started packing. He wasn't going to disappear without telling her, that would be cruel, but he wanted to take his computer gear, his gaming stuff, and she wouldn't understand that if he spun her a yarn about a few days in Spain. He'd have to pay for excess baggage, but it didn't matter, he'd have the money.

As soon as he had collected what he was owed he would book his ticket. There was probably enough in his account to cover that already, but he would wait until everything was squared away. He'd asked for the money in cash. Let Graham have the hassle of getting it and there wouldn't be any trail. He wasn't stupid. He knew they could follow a money trail through the bank. Real cash was the way to go; untraceable.

They weren't looking for him, the filth had no idea. It was obvious from the news they weren't any nearer to finding out what had happened. So, he didn't need to worry – he'd use his own passport. Last time he'd been away they'd barely looked at it anyway. He pulled it out from the back of the drawer and flipped through the pages. All empty, no visas, it was a shame. He'd been away. Spain, Holland, Belgium, Budapest for God's sake. Okay they were all short trips, stag weekends, but there was no record. Maybe after Brexit they'd start stamping passports again. That'd be cool. Ah well. He flipped to the back page – crap photograph, it made him smile. He really should have known better than to have his hair so short, it made him look like a yob.

He scanned the details. His brain refused to accept what he was seeing. He closed it, quickly, and stood looking at it. For a minute he struggled with what he'd seen. He'd made a mistake, surely. He opened it again, slowly. He held it up to the light. He ran his finger over the print. It was out of date. His passport was six bloody months out of date.

He threw it across the room where it hit the wall with a weak sort of slap and then slid to the floor. Ben sat on the edge of his bed, his head in his hands. This was absolutely typical. He had been so impressed with himself. Dealing with the problems, fixing stuff as it came along. Anyone else would have fallen to pieces when the body was found. Actually, most likely before that, when the job went bad that would have finished most people. Not him, no he just got himself together and took control. Okay, it had seemed so simple when he'd first come up with the idea but, in fairness, this wasn't everyday stuff, this was extreme and you had to be on your toes, ready to react. And he had. It had been intricate and clever, the internet side of it. He'd enjoyed setting it all up, scamming the information from her, taking her in. Making her trust him so that she opened up and told him what she was really up to. Yes, that part had been fun.

He walked across the room and kicked the little burgundy booklet into the corner. He crouched against the wall, his legs bent, his head on his knees.

He pulled out his laptop and put in a Google search. *How long will it take to renew my passport?* Weeks, it would take weeks. He scrolled and clicked. If he went to try and get it done urgently then he'd have to have a story and it would attract attention. It would mean him going in person. He'd need a new photograph. He couldn't take a selfie. His mother wouldn't be able to do it, she could barely text on her mobile. So, he'd have to ask a mate to do it. It would mean more lies, more risk.

He swore. He pulled his trainer from under the bed and flung it at the wall.

"Are you alright, love?" His mother had come in and was standing at the door. "What are you doing? Are you going away? You didn't say. What about your work?"

"Oh, Mum. Yeah. Actually, I'm going on a course. I was going to tell you. I only found out today."

"Where to?"

"What?"

"Where is the course?"

"Oh, erm. Scotland. Yeah, Edinburgh."

103

She bent and picked up his passport. She laughed. "You won't need this, will you?"

He reached to take it from her. "No, course not. It was in my suitcase."

"So, when are you going?"

"This weekend. I'll probably go on Sunday. Have a night there before the course starts."

"How long? I might ask our Doris to come and stay. You won't mind her using your room, will you?"

"No that's fine. Tell you what though, don't ask her yet, eh? I'm still waiting for the final details."

"Alright, love. Do you want a brew? I'm just putting the kettle on."

It'd calmed him down. The arrival of his mum. The need to appear normal. Okay, there was no need to panic. He'd have to change his plans. Actually, Edinburgh might even work. Oh no, better still, Ireland. Northern Ireland. He didn't need a passport for there, but it was right away, out of the country. He could go from Liverpool, easy. He smiled. He was the man, cool under fire, that was him. It'd all be okay.

Chapter 27

Terry's house was a small semi, brick-built under a tiled roof. The windows were dressed with old-fashioned net curtains, except for one on the first floor over the front door. The vertical blinds in that room were dark grey and Jordan would have put money on that being Terry's room. There was a Liverpool Football Club sticker in the window. No surprise there.

"Thanks, boss."

Terry had the door open before the car had come to a complete stop at the kerbside. A Honda motorbike was pulled up onto the pavement with a couple of young boys loitering around it. They were close enough to touch, but not actually daring to lay a hand on the shiny bodywork.

"Bugger off, Jason, go on. Don't you dare touch our Steve's bike or I'll have your guts for garters." As the kids ran away, he leaned in to collect his laptop bag. "Sorry I can't ask you in, boss. My mam's going to be in a bit of a state, not a good time."

"That's fine, Terry. I understand. But really, shouldn't you be reporting this? See if your mum needs victim support at least."

"Nah. She'll have all the support she needs, my cousin's here." He waved a hand in the direction of the motorbike. "His bird'll be with him. She'll be okay. Now I'm home she'll be fine."

"But what about her stuff, the stuff that was nicked? Her bag and whatever. At the very least she'll need a crime number if she wants to claim on her insurance."

The hint of a grin flitted across Terry's face.

"Really, boss, I've got this. I'll see you tomorrow, yeah. If you need me before then just give us a couple of hours here and then give me a bell."

He was inside the house before Jordan had reached the end of the road, the two boys flipping him the bird and mooning him as he passed. He laughed in spite of himself. Scallies they called them around here and the name suited them. He'd been a bit like that himself when he was a kid, out for mischief, nothing serious, but he must have been a darned nuisance to his neighbours. Fortunately, his mum and his gran had sorted him out and put him on the straight and narrow and the police force had finished the job.

Jordan called Penny on the hands free. Her sister was with her and they'd ordered a takeaway and were drinking wine. It sounded fun and the giggling made him lonely for his wife and his home.

"I'll be back as soon as I can, love. Sorry about this. We'll celebrate really soon and congratulations again."

"It's okay. You go and catch bad guys. Love you."

* * *

In the incident room most of the desks were empty. DC Searle leaned forward, her face lit blue white by her computer screen. She turned and smiled as Jordan came to stand beside her.

"Great work today, Rosalind. If you can stay a while, I'll need you to take me through the CCTV footage. What have you done about trying to get the driver identified?"

She blushed and shook her head. "I wasn't sure how to do it all. I didn't want to overstep the mark."

"Never do that. Never. If you think something needs doing, go ahead. If you get it wrong, there are plenty of people who'll put you right. It might be a bit uncomfortable, maybe embarrassing, but the case is the main thing. Anyway, don't worry, we'll get that sorted first thing tomorrow. You have to get onto the image retrieval officers, and they'll cut out stills and enhance them. Make sure you have all the paperwork sorted because we don't want evidence cock-ups further down the line. If you get stuck let me know, or DC Denn. With luck we'll have an idea what this driver looks like. In the meantime, let's just see what you got for me."

There was a noise in the corridor, the door opened, and Beverly Powell stood in the gap, backlit by the glow from the corridor lights.

"Do you need me, sir?"

"No, I thought you'd have gone. There was only a need for DC Searle, unless you have anything else for me?"

"No. I've updated the whiteboard."

Jordan glanced across the room. "Great. Not that much on it yet, though. Still if we get a decent image of this bloke's face, we might be onto something."

She left without another word.

Rosalind Searle raised her eyebrows. "She's rather intense, boss. She told me off earlier for using the wrong colour marker to label the picture of the van. She's got different coloured pins and a list on the board for how we are supposed to use them."

"Hmm. No harm in being organised though, eh?" Jordan said. He wasn't about to criticise the woman, but she was hard-going. Still, she got the job done.

"Yeah."

"Anyway, your footage."

Chapter 28

Graham had known it was going to be difficult and he had known that he couldn't tell Rose everything. He could never tell anyone everything. He had started with an admission about the five thousand.

"But hang on, who is this bloke? Why did you give him money?"

Graham sighed and rubbed his hands over his face. He poured some more gin and then saw the look on her face. Rose was struggling with the no alcohol part of being pregnant. He needed it though and he gulped it back in one mouthful. He felt the edges of his anxiety soften and blur.

"Okay, let me start again at the beginning. Come on, sit down."

She shook her head, wouldn't move from where she stood, in front of his chair, glowering down at him. She had cupped the small swell of her belly in her hands. He had noticed her doing this now and then. It was sweet normally, but today it just added to the shame. His child was in there and right now, when he should have been securing their future, he was screwing everything up. He tried again.

"Okay. This bloke, he says his name is Ben, but I don't know – it probably isn't that. He said that he works for a tracing site. Online, you know. A place where people go to try and find long lost relatives." She didn't respond. "Well, he said there was a woman who was trying to trace me, sent me a letter with some document copies in. He said that she was out to cause trouble. He said that if I paid him, he would make it go away. Warn her off or something – I don't know, I didn't ask what he was going to do."

"But who was she? I don't get this, Graham, who the hell was she and why was she trying to trace you? What trouble could she cause?"

"I don't know. I'd never heard of her."

It wasn't a complete lie. He hadn't known of her, not really, though it had been there, in the back of his mind.

"In that case why did you pay him money? Why didn't you just tell him to sod off and then if she got in touch, you just tell her you don't know who she is? You're not usually this daft, Graham. How could you be taken in like this, by some scam artist? Who did she say she was, if she even exists?"

He didn't know how far to go. This slope was very slippery and once he set foot on it everything could slide away from him.

"Right, she said that she was a relative. You know, a long-lost relative tracing her family. That sort of thing."

"So, what was the problem, then? I mean, you always said you don't have any family, as far as you're aware. Is there someone? An old aunty or something. A cousin you knew when you were a kid. Actually yeah – maybe that would have been nice. With the baby coming. An aunty or something, just someone from your side. Ask him for the money back. Tell him you don't care. Not only that, report him to his boss. I bet he's not supposed to do that."

He had to say more.

"I don't think I can ask for the money back and he wants more now. He wants me to give him more and I've arranged to send it, transfer it, you know."

Now she did sit down. She perched on the edge of the settee, leaning forward, her arms on her knees.

"What? This doesn't make sense, not at all. Why would you do that? Why on earth would you give money, our money, away over something like this? If she's a long lost relative, why wouldn't you want to see someone from your family? I would have thought that would be exciting."

"Actually, she's probably not, is she? Really, Rose, I don't think she can be."

"Maybe not, but that's okay. We can just tell her we're not interested and if she bothers you again, you'll report her to the police. Do you know what, Graham? You've been a bloody idiot. You've thrown our money away and now you want to waste more. No, tell this bloke to eff off and if the woman is a fraud then we'll send her packing as well."

"I can't."

She stared at him, waiting for more. He had known all along that it would come to this. It had to.

"She said she's my daughter."

"What! But that's ridiculous. That's stupid, why would you even listen to him?"

There was a pause and then Rose whispered, "Graham, why would you believe that?" There was a moment of dark silence and then he heard a sob. "Oh my God."

The stress, fear, shame and horror of the last few days broke through now and he dissolved in tears, his shoulders shook and in no time, he was struggling to breathe.

He felt her move away, as he looked up she was disappearing into the hallway, her feet pounded on the stairs and the bedroom door slammed, reverberating through the whole place.

Graham sat back in the chair; his eyes closed. Christ, what was he going to do now? He had told her half a story, not even that really and it hadn't helped. He heard her coming back down the stairs and went to speak to her. She had an overnight bag in her hand. She turned to him and her ravaged face tore him apart.

"What are you doing?"

"I'm going to our Jenny's. I need to think."

Before he could move towards her, she was gone.

Chapter 29

The team was in early, all of them. Jordan had given the civilians the option, but as they were all on flexible time contracts, they were more than happy to turn up. Nobody wanted to be the one who was at home with the kids when the breakthrough happened.

DC Searle had sent the CCTV footage to the image team but while they waited for the stills to come back everyone was focused on the screens, watching the white van and then the driver, as he walked to the pub. They all hoped to spot something that would be useful.

"DC Denn, I need you to go with DC Searle and talk to the landlord as soon as we have a picture to show them. This guy was in there for a couple of hours, but he might be a regular or at least he might have been noticed. He came out of there late. We don't know for certain he is our killer, but at the very least he climbed in that van and drove away through quite a heavily populated area. If he was up to no good, he would have been careful not to attract attention. If he was just a punter passing time, then it's a bit odd. There are better ways to spend an evening than some scuzzy little boozer in Walton on your own."

There was the low hum of voices as the footage was discussed and dissected but there was no point trying to hurry things along. Jordan went through his messages and ordered some flowers for Penny. She had been in bed by the time he'd arrived home the night before, stirring as he slid under the duvet and wrapped his arms around her. They didn't have a chance to discuss her news and he felt bad. He had left her eating breakfast with her sister, who had stayed over, while Harry spread porridge over his face and anything else within reach.

The images popped into his feed as he was finalising the card payment, so he was one of the last to see them. Beverly Powell was standing by the printer, tapping her fingernails against the plastic as the printout made its way through the rollers.

There were three pictures, one from the van stopped at the traffic lights, the face obscured by reflections on the glass but the colours of the driver's jacket and hat clearly visible. The best one was him leaving the pub. He had a hat pulled low over his forehead, his hood up and a scarf around his neck, pulled up to his chin. There was just enough of his face visible to have a good idea of his features.

Jordan grinned at Rosalind Searle.

"Well done, Detective Constable. This is really going to help. Fingers crossed, we are onto something at last. We'll have his image circulated as quickly as possible on the force Facebook pages and Twitter feeds, and I'm going to have a word with DCI Cross about a feature on the television news. We need as much publicity as we can manage with this. Okay, keep me informed if there are any further sightings that look promising. Anything at all, don't hold back, people."

"Right, boss. We're off to Walton," Terry said. "We'll ask at the pub and the shops round about, just in case. We'll have a word with that old bloke that lives next door and any of the neighbours that are in."

"Excellent. I'll see if there is any chance of a few more uniforms to spread the load but do what you can for now. What happened to your hand, Terry?"

The young officer glanced down at his bruised and scabby knuckles.

"It's nothing, boss. Fell against a hard surface. It'll be fine."

Jordan watched as he walked to the door, he was limping very slightly, and his shoulders were stiff. *That was some fall.*

Chapter 30

Rose wouldn't answer his calls. Even her sister's phone went to voicemail. There was nothing to be gained from sitting in the darkened living room, so Graham went upstairs. Over and over again he replayed the events of the last few weeks. He tried and failed to see what he could have done differently. Of course, he could just have brazened it out. Faced it squarely. The repercussions of that would have been horrendous. His career, his reputation, and his marriage all in tatters. Now though, he could see that was happening anyway. Plus, he was down by five thousand pounds, Rose had left him and there was the other thing. Really the worst thing. The dead girl.

He scrolled through the news reports on the internet. It was like picking a scab, he just couldn't let it go. He hadn't done this. If he had known, if he'd had any idea, then he would have been against it completely. Of course he would. So then, he couldn't be held responsible, could he? This was all that bloke Ben's doing.

He went into the bathroom for a pee before getting into bed. He saw the pills in the bathroom cabinet. He knew that it didn't take as many painkillers as you might imagine to do the job, but it was an unreliable way to end it. He could finish up in hospital with liver failure. He couldn't put Rose through that. There were razor blades in the cabinet, and he took one out and held it between his fingers. Pushed it against the skin of his wrist. The whole idea of it, the blood, the pain, made him shudder. The thing was, he didn't want to die, he didn't want to hurt himself. He wanted to go back to the way things had been before he had ever had the letter telling him about the girl.

Beatrice.

As he allowed himself to think of her name, he gasped – it made her real. He didn't want her to be real, couldn't afford that. No. He was still trying to convince himself that she wasn't even connected to him, that it was all a mistake. Though, actually, the stuff included with the letter had left little doubt. Ben had even included a cutting from the papers back then. Back when it had happened. The account of the woman. The fact that she had withdrawn her accusations. No names, not then, but Ben had found him, somehow. Did that mean that somewhere there were documents with his name on?

There shouldn't have been anything with his name on. He hadn't been to court, and the police report should have been locked away. Surely it should have been destroyed by now. Maybe not, he didn't know. But if not that, then how? The only other way was personal contact. The girl herself. Beatrice's mother. She must have said his name. Though he hadn't allowed himself to think of her for all these years, she had been there, a vague shadow in his mind. She had been a bit older than him. She would be in her late forties now, probably. He didn't know where she was, or where she had gone after she had withdrawn her accusations and run away from the gossip and the speculation. But she knew his name, she wouldn't have forgotten it, same as he never forgot hers.

Vera.

A slag they had called her. A drunken whore. Always in the pub, skirts too short, tops too tight. It had been true that she was out for a good time. Yes, she drank to excess. Yes, she flirted. But what he had done, the thing that she hadn't had the strength to demand justice for, was unforgiveable. That was back when he had been using drugs, drinking too much, and was out of control. Back then he had ruined someone's life. He had waited for the reckoning and when it hadn't come, he had moved on. Apart from the nub of guilt that he carried, always. It was a vile sort of comeuppance that it had emerged now when life was so good and it was going to ruin everything for him.

Unless he could sort this out, Vera was going to get her justice after all.

Chapter 31

Jordan was struggling to keep control. DCI Cross was simply flexing his virtual muscle and they both knew it. It was pointless, stupid really and very wrong.

"You don't have any real proof that this bloke, the driver of the white van, is our murderer. You know as well as I do that, in most of these cases, it turns out to be the boyfriend, or indeed the girlfriend, husband – whatever. That's where you should be looking."

As he spoke the chief constable lifted the photograph and wagged it in the air.

"This could just be some poor bloke passing a lonely night. You want me to stick his picture all over the television, nationwide mind you. I don't think so. You need to bring me something more than just the fact that he didn't overtake a bus and then hung around in Walton."

"But, sir, with respect, we have had no indication of a partner, or boyfriend, no regular visitors to the house, no mention of anyone where this woman worked. This man was seen driving into the road where our victim lived and then leaving some time later, just around the estimated time of the murder. His behaviour is suspicious, even his appearance is that of someone trying to hide his identity.

The number plate on the van is obscured by dirt. Sir, I truly believe that this is a person of interest and we need to identify him, as quickly as possible, and the television has been proven to be the most successful means many times."

"Yes, and the reason it's so successful is that we are really careful about what we feature. This is too vague, and this bloke would be very likely to sue us when we find out that he is actually just some poor sod who had a row with the wife and needed to pass an evening away from the nagging. No, Detective Inspector. I'm happy with you putting it on the internet, doesn't cost much in manpower, but not the television. It isn't worth it. Not until you have more evidence. I've been in the job a lot longer than you have, DI Carr. You mark my words, you need to look for the boyfriend. Now then, was there anything else?"

"I would like an all ports alert on the van, sir. We are putting this out there and if he sees it, which is very possible, then he may try and run."

"Okay, that's fine. Probably a waste of time but go for it. At least it'll give me something to tell Campbell and there's been precious little up to now."

"Thank you, sir."

Jordan felt his fingernails digging into the palms of his hands, but he smiled as he turned and left. He managed to maintain his composure all the way to the end of the corridor where he took out his frustration on an innocent waste bin, which never recovered from being kicked down the staircase.

By the time he was back in the incident room he had gathered himself together.

"Right, it's been decided that, for the moment, we are sticking with the internet, so I need you all focused. Anything at all that might give us more ammunition."

He regretted the choice of words immediately, it gave away the real situation; he carried on.

"We need more evidence against this bloke. I feel there is enough to make him a suspect. Right place, right time for the crime. He appears to be following the bus and afterwards he is heading down towards the river. It would be useful if we could see him in Liverpool earlier so, can a couple of you go back to the CCTV of Beatrice? Now we have this it could be that he'll be easier to spot. Okay. Jake and Tony, can you do that? The rest of you are monitoring emails and messages. Everyone clear?"

There was a mumble of agreement and he left them to it. Back at his desk he updated his book and then reviewed the footage again. It wasn't much more than gut feeling, but many times he'd been advised not to ignore that. *The best coppers have it and trust it,'* he'd been told and, though he would never describe himself as the best, he knew he was good. He needed a conversation with this man, soon.

Chapter 32

Ben pulled the remaining cheap phone from his pocket, his last burner. He dialled Graham's number, copying it from the piece of paper. He hit the wrong key twice and had to start again. It was all these little things that were winding him up. They didn't tell you all of this, on the telly they just skimmed over it. Of course, that was make-believe, this was real. He wasn't some namby-pamby actor – he was the real thing.

Being honest, he never imagined it would have come to this but it was her own fault it had ended this way. Still, he was dealing with it.

Graham didn't answer right away, it took three tries.

"Yes?"

He sounded hesitant and nervous. The thought of Graham so scared that he didn't even want to answer the phone made Ben smile.

"Have you got me the money?"

"I've arranged it, yes. It's in a bank account. I set one up separately. If you give me your details, I'll transfer it."

"Ha – I don't think so. You must think I'm some sort of divvy. No, I want cash. All of it."

"How do you expect me to do that? It's Saturday. The banks are closed. I can't get that sort of money out of a hole in the wall."

Ben was speechless for a couple of seconds. He hadn't thought it through.

"How much can you get?"

"Five hundred."

"That's no bloody use. I told you I want it in cash. I'll give you until Monday, you'll have to get it for me by then. Otherwise I'm sending my trace research to your wife, your boss and, oh yes, and just for good measure, the papers, might even start a whole new Facebook page for it. Ask for votes on whether or not you should have got away with it. You'll be stuffed."

"Don't be stupid. I can't get ten thousand pounds just like that. You have to order it, make arrangements. You've never dealt with this sort of money, have you?"

Ben's anger ratchetted up. He had screwed up and now this shithead was treating him like some sort of idiot.

"Don't call me stupid, it's not me in this mess. This isn't my problem, la. This is on you. I'll ring you on Monday morning."

He clicked off the phone, kicked out at a plastic drink bottle lying in the gutter. Now he'd have to hang around until Monday at least. He thought he'd have been in Ireland by tomorrow afternoon. He took the SIM out of the phone, dropped it into a drain and stamped on the plastic handset.

This was Graham's fault, the rapist, the dirty low life, sex offender. It was his job to sort this. But what if he couldn't get the money? Even if Ben carried out the threat and dropped the bloke right in the shit, he still needed to get away. Graham didn't know who Ben was, but the police would be able to work it backwards, trace him. He couldn't risk it, they'd find him double quick. But he couldn't go with the measly five thousand. That wouldn't last more than a couple of weeks. He sat on the wall outside the church hall. His mum was inside the building opposite, playing bingo. The thought of his mother, a bit dibby, it had to be said, living her small life, just plodding on from day to day gave him an idea.

He went home. It didn't take him long to research online bank accounts. His skills on the computer were what had secured him the job with Time Tracers. It was how he'd been able to set up the scam to track the girl. He was ace on the internet.

He knew his mum had never had a driving licence but a couple of years before she had gone with her sister for a week in Marbella. She hadn't been impressed – food too foreign, the shops weren't what she was used to, and she didn't like flying. But it did mean she had a passport.

She'd be home in just over an hour. He went straight to her bedroom. He didn't often go into her room and he had a moment of guilt. This was her private space. It smelled of talcum powder and deodorant. He screwed up his face as he opened her underwear drawer and pushed his hand under her big knickers and beige bras. But he knew from past experience that it was where she hid her bits of jewellery and spare cash. Sure enough it was in there along with a couple of insurance policies.

Once he had the ID, it didn't take him long to open an account. He loved the internet. He had to transfer a few hundred but that wouldn't look odd, just a thoughtful son bailing his mother out of her gambling debts.

He wouldn't ring that Graham yet. He needed a couple of new SIM cards anyway. He could get them from the offy. Let him sweat for a bit, let him have a sleepless night. But then tomorrow he could make the transfer. Okay, he had hoped to make the money untraceable, but this was good. Nobody would look at his mum and she would never know there was an account in her name with thousands in it. He took the passport back and replaced it. As he left the room, he felt a sudden sort of longing. She'd be sad when he went, and he wouldn't be able to tell her where he was or how long he would be gone for. For a moment he wished for life as it had been before. Then he remembered the money. It wasn't forever, once things had calmed down, he'd be back and next time he'd be more careful.

Chapter 33

Graham hadn't bothered to get dressed. He had made tea and eaten a slice of bread and jam. Then that Ben had rung, and he had spewed it all back into the toilet pan. He tried to sound calm, unflustered, but inside his stomach was churning and the pounding in his chest was painful. That would be an answer, a bloody heart attack and finish it all decently. Rose would get the insurance. The threat would disappear, and he wouldn't have to struggle any longer.

It hadn't happened and now he was sitting in the living room, the curtains still drawn. He had to get his hands on the money. He couldn't get cash, not that quickly. Given a few days he could, but not by Monday. He'd get a couple of thousand, take that, and tell the bloke that he'd get the rest as soon as he could.

He heard Rose's car pull into the drive and dashed to the front door to meet her. She was haggard and ill-looking, there were dark shadows under her eyes, and they were puffy and sore. She had been crying and he was riddled with guilt as he looked at her. This was no good for her, in her condition.

She didn't push him away as he put his arms gently around her shoulders and shepherded her into the hallway.

"Rose," he said, "I'm sorry. I'm so sorry. I never wanted to upset you like this."

She pulled away and looked at him. He didn't see forgiveness, but more resignation, as though she had always expected him to let her down and now here it was.

"We need to talk, Graham. You need to tell me all about this and then we'll have to see what we can do."

"What did your sister say?"

"Jesus, Graham, I didn't tell Jenny about this. I just told her we'd had a row. I couldn't tell her about this. We can't tell anyone about this."

"No, that's it. That's why I didn't say anything."

"Get me a glass of water and then we'll sort it."

He didn't respond. She thought this was a minor thing, the appearance of an unknown daughter. Shocking, perhaps even devastating but manageable. Something that you could adjust to and, in time, even accept. That might have been an option if he hadn't panicked, but not now.

He didn't know what he was going to tell her. He would need to come up with something, but every option just threw up more questions. He could just tell her to leave it to him, that he was dealing with it and she didn't need to give it any more thought. He knew that wouldn't wash. One of the things that had attracted him to her was her strength, her determination. She was quite a lot younger than him, but she took things on the chin and then sorted them. He used to say she was like a terrier with a bone. He wouldn't be able to flannel her, but he had to keep her at arm's length from the truth.

When he came into the living room, she had thrown her jacket on the settee beside her. She took the water and then stared ahead at the chair beside the fireplace. The message was clear, he wasn't to sit near her, he wasn't to come too close.

"Right. I want the truth from you, Graham. All of it. I have had time to think this through and I am beginning to get my head round it all. This is not as big a problem as it seemed at first. Okay, I was shocked, horrified to be honest. But then, I always knew you had a life before me. I didn't give it a lot of thought because I imagined you'd told me all I needed to know. Seems I was a fool there."

She held up a hand as Graham opened his mouth to speak.

"No, don't say anything. Not yet. If this is true, that you have a daughter then… fair enough. I can accept that. I am brassed off that you never told me, of course I am, but I can accept it. I can just about believe that you didn't know – just about. What I can't understand is why you lied. Why you spent our money to hide it from me and why you are letting yourself be blackmailed. I thought our marriage was strong, Graham. I thought we had something special. I was wrong. If that was true you would have told me about this. Anyway, we need to just deal with it now. You need to tell this bloke to sod off and you need to let this girl contact you and then we'll decide whether or not we let her into our lives. You see, when you break it all down, the problem is not that big. We will not let this ruin us, ruin everything we've worked for. This baby will have both parents and a happy home. I told you right at the start. I grew up in a broken marriage and that is not happening with my child. There is no other option. It's you who has complicated it, threatened it. So, who was she?"

"Who do you mean?"

"Who do you think? Who is this girl's mother and why didn't you know that you had a daughter, if that's true? To be honest I am yet to be convinced."

Chapter 34

Where the hours after a prime-time news article would have seen the incident room swamped with calls, the reaction to the social media appeal was much more muted.

Now and again one of the civilians would laugh or curse as they scrolled through the messages, but Jordan felt the frustration in the room because they were receiving so little useful feedback.

"Why did we not go with the television appeal, boss?" Terry asked.

"Decision taken higher up."

"Right, but– I mean, like, why? It's a bit odd. We'd have such a better response. We'd have had loads of calls by now."

"Yeah, I know, but let's just make the best of it. Anyway, tell me what you found out in Walton."

"Not much, I'm afraid. The barman at the pub recognised the guy in picture but he has no idea who the bloke is. Hadn't ever seen him before, or since for that matter. He sat on his own, had a couple of pints of shandy that lasted all night and then went out alone. All stuff that we knew or guessed. None of the neighbours had seen him before and the old bloke next door was absolutely adamant that Beatrice never had people calling round, no cars parked outside. No parties, nothing."

Beverly Powell strode across the room carrying a sheet of paper.

"I've printed this out, sir."

Jordan was about to give her the 'saving paper' speech again but couldn't be bothered. He just wanted some action.

"Long story short, this woman – Mrs Susan Blakely – is a bit of an internet addict, hence her presence on the Facebook page, I guess. Anyway, she is tracing her family history and was looking at sites that offer help. She is convinced that the van driver is one of the 'tracers' from one of these sites, 'timetracers.com'."

"Okay, and?"

"I had a look and, here we are." She held out the paper. "He does look similar, I have to say. No hat of course and I think this man appears younger. Anyway, I have the address. They are based on the Wirral. I Googled the office and actually it's just a house. So, perhaps it's all done remotely. Means that we'll have to find out from them where this bloke lives. Shall I go ahead and contact them?"

"This is brilliant work, Beverly. Really great. However, contacting the company would probably be better coming from us. You know, from serving officers and done in person. I know you're keen, which is great, but we have to be careful that we don't confuse roles."

He smiled as he said it, but he saw her face freeze.

Terry may have meant well but his intervention didn't help.

"You know, Bev, you could sign up. Why don't you look into joining the force as an officer? I mean, you might be pushing the upper age limit for a recruit, but with your experience they'd probably make allowances."

There was a hush in the room, Jordan was aware of sidelong glances from the people at the nearest desks. To give her credit, Beverly didn't respond. He saw a sparkle of moisture in her eyes, but she simply turned and walked away.

"If I can do anything else, just let me know," she murmured, her back ramrod straight as she left the room. One of the other women scurried after her.

"Sorry." Terry held up his hands. "That didn't come out quite as I meant it to."

"Never mind. Let's just get out of here and go and see this bloke on the Wirral."

This could come back to bite them, Jordan knew. If she put in a complaint of ageism or something, it would cause problems and he just didn't need it. Not with the case stalled and DCI Cross on his back.

"We'll take my car," Jordan said. "No need to pay twice for the tunnel. I know it's only a couple of pounds but still. Anyway, you look as though you could do with a rest. That must have been quite a 'fall against a hard object' that you had."

Terry flexed his fist and looked down as the scabs on his knuckles oozed a little.

"Aye. These hard objects can be buggers, boss."

"Terry, if you're serious about your career you have to remember that we uphold the law, we're not above it."

"Don't know what you're getting at, boss," Terry said as he slid stiffly into the passenger seat.

Chapter 35

"You said you'd give me until Monday." Graham had answered the phone quickly. He didn't want Rose to hear it and come down from the bedroom.

"Changed my mind," Ben said.

"I haven't got the money. I told you I wouldn't be able to get it."

"Yeah. And I decided to help you out."

"What do you mean?"

"I'm going to let you transfer the money. I've decided to let you off the hook. I'll text you the details. Get it to me before tomorrow."

He wasn't sure why he did it. Maybe he didn't want to be told what to do anymore, maybe he wanted to feel that he was in control of something.

"No," Graham said. "Tell you what, I can get two thousand, in cash. I'll bring that to you tomorrow and then I'll transfer the rest as soon as I can."

There was a short pause and then the chance of cash in hand proved too tempting for Ben.

"Okay. I'll ring you in the morning and tell you where to meet me. You'd better be on your own. Don't try any funny business or believe me, mate, you'll be so deep in shit you'll never get out."

It hadn't occurred to Graham to do anything other than take the money and hand it over. He wanted to see who this man was though. The more he thought about it, the more important it was. Otherwise he knew he would be tormented. He imagined walking down the street, hearing a voice, seeing someone walking towards him and wondering: *Is that the man?*

Rose came down from the bedroom where she'd been having a lie-down. She looked drawn and pale. She didn't smile as she threw herself into the chair by the fire.

Graham went to kneel in front of her.

"How are you feeling, love?"

"I don't know, Graham. I just don't know. I feel betrayed and sad. I feel frustrated and I am furious with you. Absolutely livid. I don't understand why you couldn't have told me. I know it's a big thing, you having a daughter, but why couldn't you have told me? I think that's what hurts the most. I don't know whether I'll ever be able to get past that."

"What can I do?"

She shook her head. "I don't know. I feel hollowed out, as if you've taken everything. I think you should tell me as much as you can. It might be easier to handle if I know all the facts. Who was this woman? How long were you with her? Why did you finish with her?"

"It wasn't like that, Rose. It really wasn't. We never had a relationship. We weren't an item. Not like that."

"So, it was just a quick screw, is that it? You had a oneser with her and she got pregnant and never told you? Really? That seems a bit farfetched."

"Yes, it was a bit like that."

"How do you mean, 'a bit like that'?"

He was worn out. The worry and the fear had him at the end of his tether and that was the only reason he did what he did. After all these years, this one moment pushed him over the edge. The look in her eyes, her pale face and the disbelief in her voice. All of that and he had taken all he could. So, he held her hands in his. Time had run out for him, he was going to have to come clean no matter what. He closed his eyes for a moment and then he told her.

Chapter 36

Bromborough was like most places on the Wirral, a mixture of affluence and struggle. As it happened the address that Beverly had given them was in an area that seemed affluent.

The house was at the edge of the town, on an estate that had the look of ex-council. But it was well kept: grass verges neatly trimmed, clean, late-model cars parked on flagged driveways, and many of the homes had been extended and improved.

"This is nice," Terry said. "I wonder how expensive it is to buy here?"

"Not a clue, mate," Jordan said. "Must pay quite well, though, this tracing business."

Their knock on the door was answered by a man in casual clothes, wearing horn-rimmed glasses and with a pen in his hand. They both had their warrant cards open and visible. He glanced at them and raised his eyebrows.

"Problem?" he said.

"I don't think so, sir. I'm Detective Inspector Jordan Carr and this is DC Terry Denn. We are with the Merseyside Police. Sorry to bother you at the weekend but

I wonder if you have a few minutes? We need to talk to you about one of your employees."

"Hello, I'm Stan Lipscowe." The man held out his hand to shake theirs. "An employee?"

"Yes. This is the address we have for timetracers.com?" Jordan put a question in his voice.

"Yes. That's me, but my people don't work here." He turned his head to look into the hallway behind him. "We all work from home. No need for a central office. We're internet-based."

"Yes, I get that, sir. In fact, that's possibly all we need from you. The address of a Ben Harwood. He is a member of your staff, I think?"

"Yes, yes Ben works for me. Sorry, look come in, won't you?"

"Thank you. We'll try not to take up too much of your time."

"It's okay. Is Ben alright? I mean, I know he's off sick right now, but I thought it was his back trouble again."

"We just need a word with him. We're hoping he can help us with some enquiries."

"Oh, fair enough. He's located over the water, in Liverpool. I've met him once or twice. I like to know who my people are, but most of our meetings are online. Anyway, just come through into the office."

They walked through the house and into the area that had been the attached garage. It was now a decent-sized office space. There were four computers on a long worktable and an air conditioning unit buzzed in the background. Along one wall were bookshelves filled with reference books, mostly history. It was neat and tidy.

"Impressive," said Terry.

"Thanks. I think it helps to have a proper place to work. Helps you to concentrate. I try to encourage the 'tracers' to do the same but of course they can't all manage it. Ben works from his bedroom I think, but he does a good job. It's a bit of a gift. We can all search for stuff on the internet, but you have to have an open mind, go down avenues you wouldn't expect. It's getting easier with more stuff being put online but now and then you have to use the library, that sort of thing. He's been a quick learner and as I say he has the gift for it. I have people all over the country. What we try to do is work with people who are tracing in their own areas. That way if you do need to move out of the office, out of the digital world as it were, it cuts down on travel. I try to offer a service that is a bit different. More human, if that makes sense."

"Do you know him well?"

"No, he's only been with me for about eighteen months. Before that he worked in a call centre as far as I know. Don't know very much about him. He's not married. Lives with his mum. That's about it. Anyway, I hope he can help you. Don't you go poaching him away from me now."

Stan handed them a sticky note with an address scrawled across it.

"He's off sick, you say?" Terry asked.

"Yes, sent me an email a day or two ago. He's decided to take some leave. We're pretty flexible, this sort of work doesn't have to be done nine to five. If I need him, I can find him no matter where he is."

"How closely do you monitor his work? Would you know who he was, erm, 'tracing'?"

"Of course. It would be someone 'seeking' at least in the north of England and where possible within a fifty-mile radius."

"Could we have that information?"

Before Jordan finished speaking Stan Lipscowe was shaking his head.

"Out of the question, totally, I'm afraid. We offer complete confidentiality. Of course, if you were to have a warrant or whatever we'd never be deliberately difficult, but without that, no. Sorry."

They could have pushed it, data protection didn't apply once someone was dead, and anyway they knew a warrant would be relatively easy to obtain, but for the moment they wanted this man on their side. They also wanted to avoid giving too much away.

"If we need anything else from you, we'll be in touch," Jordan said.

"Here, take my card. Might save you coming over. Zoom or Skype, anything like that I'm happy to meet up."

Jordan thanked him and he and Terry headed out to the car.

"Okay, Bootle it is then. Balliol Road," Jordan said as they returned to the car. "The tunnel will be quickest."

Chapter 37

The Mersey Tunnel was busy with weekend traffic streaming back from North Wales, but in just over half an hour they were in the rabbit warren of residential streets that is Bootle.

"Thank heavens for satnavs," Jordan said, as they pulled up to the kerb outside Ben Harwood's house.

They assumed that the woman who answered the door was his mother and couldn't miss the sneer as they held up their warrant cards.

"Mrs Harwood?" Jordan smiled at her but there was no change in her expression, which was cold and defensive.

"What do you want?"

"Just a quick word with your son, if we could, ma'am?"

"Not here."

"Is he not? Do you know where he is?"

"No."

"Any idea how long he'll be? We really do need to have a word. We were led to believe he wasn't so well. Trouble with his back," Terry said.

"Aye well, you were led to believe wrong. There's nothing wrong with my Ben so somebody's been telling porkies, haven't they? He's not here and I'm going out with my sister so, if you don't mind."

She began to push the door closed and Jordan had no choice but to place a hand on the white UPVC.

She glared at him. "Let go. I'm in a hurry."

"I'm sorry, ma'am, but we really do need to know where your son is. We're investigating a serious crime and we believe he may be able to help us."

"You're unlucky then, he's not here. He's away on a course. He's got a very clever job and they've sent him off to do a course."

She tilted her chin as she spoke and, for Jordan, the glint of pride in her eyes was heartrending. Of course, he may not be a murderer, but having just left his boss, they already knew he was a liar.

"Mrs Harwood, we need to have a look at Ben's room and if necessary, we can get a warrant. You really don't want that, do you? You really don't want a hoard of bobbies tramping through your house."

"You can't look at his room, our Doris is up there. She's come to stay for a bit, while our Ben's away. Keeping me company. So there, you can bugger off now."

"We'll be back later. You could have made this easier, but we'll be back."

Terry shook his head as he spoke and then, with no other option they turned away and walked to the car. Jordan was already on his phone calling DCI Cross at home. Making apologies and asking to have a warrant requested.

"Not much more we can do tonight, Terry. She's not going to give us anything, is she?"

"Don't reckon so. Looking a bit promising though, him lying to his mother."

"Yeah. We've got an all-ports organised on his vehicle so let's hope he hasn't ditched that and got himself some other transport. Bloody frustrating though. I mean, if she really believes he's just on a work thing, why won't she let us in?"

"Goes against the grain, doesn't it, helping us?"

"With a bit of luck, he doesn't know we're looking for him, so providing he's still driving that white van, the ANPR will pick him up. He shouldn't be able to get out of the country. I'll drop you at home if you like, pick you up in the morning."

"No, you're okay. Just let me out at the bus stop. I'm going for a bevvy anyway, so I don't need my car."

"Are you sure? It's no trouble."

"Wrong direction, boss. Honest, it's fine."

"Okay. Early start tomorrow. We really need to be moving this along."

Jordan called into the supermarket on the way back to Crosby, picked up a bottle of Penny's favourite wine and a chocolate cake. It wasn't the meal out he was planning for the future, when this case was over, but it made her smile.

Chapter 38

Ben had felt quite emotional leaving home. His mum had been excited, thinking he was off to Scotland for his job.

"I expect they'll be promoting you soon."

She didn't understand how things worked these days, but he smiled, bent and gave her a kiss.

He'd watched in the rear-view mirror as he drove away. She stood outside on the pavement waving until he reached the corner and he knew she would stay a while longer. She'd be hoping a neighbour would see her and ask where he was going.

He'd give her a ring once he was in Ireland. He had been away before, of course he had, but this – not knowing when he would see her again – was harder than he thought it would be. He didn't welcome the next thought, the one about the woman in Newcastle, the one whose daughter would never be coming home. Well, it didn't matter. As far as he'd been able to find out she was out of it anyway. Away with the fairies. The emails had been brief, but that, about the mother, was one thing that he'd been told, that she was dying and that was why she had blurted out secrets.

So, the girl had wanted to meet her biological father, not for an emotional reveal, but to find out the truth, to confront him. It was like something out of a book. He had never spoken to her on the phone. It was discouraged by the company, but once he'd had the first couple of messages, once she'd started to unburden herself, he'd known this was his big chance and he would be able to put his plan into action.

The idea of making a bit on the side had been there ever since he began working for Stan Lipscowe. After all, he'd thought, why not? Not everyone tracing their family was doing it so they could brag about being related to some Lord or Duke or something. It had only been a question of time before someone with different intent had come forward. And why should they be allowed to come in and mess up people's lives? That wasn't right. In the end he was performing a service. At least he would have been if it hadn't gone tits up.

Contacting people directly and offering to warn customers off was definitely against company policy. He'd marked the contact as failed and sent it to the rejected folder. He'd deleted the other stuff from his own machine as well. He knew the police could retrieve deleted information from hard drives so just in case, he would replace his when he had the chance. Probably when he got to Ireland. He could get a new one on the internet, he didn't need to replace the whole computer. For now, though, it looked innocent enough at first glance, just gaming and shopping.

That Stan Lipscowe was missing a trick, he hadn't realised the potential of his business. All they were supposed to do was send back a family tree and notes on any interesting ancestors. A couple of hundred pounds a pop, it was nothing. Three or four emails was all it usually took. But there was a lot more you could do once you got to know what was in people's past.

He needed to keep his job though, that was vital. Maybe later he could set up on his own, but he didn't want to shell out for advertising and whatnot right now. So, he'd email the boss and say he was still willing to work, even though he was officially off sick. In a day or two when he'd sorted this hiccup.

With the girl, careful questioning had given him his chance. He'd made her think he was sympathetic. What she wanted, she'd said, was to find out the truth – was she really the result of rape? She was coming to the area, she told him. If he didn't help her then she'd have to do it on her own. He thought she was still hanging on to the idea that her mother had lost her marbles and imagined things in the past that hadn't happened. But he could tell that there was enough doubt there to keep her searching. It hadn't been that difficult to find the report in the paper. The charges had been dropped but that didn't mean there was no record of the incident, you just needed to know where to look. It was easy to do the sums. Nine months is so specific, and it was helpful that they noted it was the Sexual Offences Act.

Anyway, he didn't know what she'd intended to do with the information, but it stood to reason that Graham wouldn't want this to come out. The guy must have thought he'd dodged the bullet. The charges had been dropped prior to the conclusion of the investigation but there was enough to cause him problems, especially in the current climate.

Bloody shame really, no need for it to have become so complicated. There had been no need for her to end up dead. When he did allow himself to think about that, he had to admit that he'd simply lost control. It wasn't his fault, just the way things panned out really. Not premeditated, that's what they'd say – so not murder. Maybe manslaughter. But they'd have to catch him first and they hadn't a clue. Well, he hadn't seen the news for a day or two, not with sorting everything at home. He needed to have a look later, when he had a minute.

He had to keep his head down for a bit and then he'd have another go. There had to be big money in it. He wasn't giving up after one job. Next time he'd ask for a lot more – a hell of a lot more just in case things went pear-shaped again.

Now he had to find somewhere to stay. Probably best in the city centre, somewhere busy with lots of passing trade. He'd blend in with the visitors. He knew there were some down by the Pier Head. Then he could meet Graham, get the cash and be off on the ferry to Belfast. Sorted. He was looking forward to the sail.

It was only as he was standing at the reception desk that he wondered about the wisdom of using his own name. He thought, paying cash, he wouldn't have to worry, but the pimply kid behind the desk insisted on seeing 'some form of identification'.

Ben tried arguing.

"I'm paying cash, mate."

"Yes, sir, but it's company policy. It's for our records."

"Why?" Ben said.

"I'm not really sure I understand."

"Why do you need to see ID? You can see me. I'm standing right in front of you and I'm giving you money. For Christ's sake I'm only staying one night."

"Sorry, sir. Company policy."

"You're a bit of a jobsworth, aren't you?"

"I can call the manager, if you like." The lad reached for the phone.

This was getting out of control and the last thing he needed was to draw attention to himself.

"No, look… Here take it." He held out his driving licence and watched as the receptionist made a note on the computer.

Ben wondered if he was going to have to shell out to get fake papers after all. He wasn't sure how you'd do it but maybe he'd have to find out. He couldn't surf the dark web from here, not on a public Wi-Fi system but when he got to Ireland, found somewhere to stay, then he'd have to look into it. He'd have a couple of nights in Belfast. A bed and breakfast though. They wouldn't be asking to see his driving licence, not if he offered them cash. Then he'd rent something, a flat, a caravan maybe – near the coast.

He reached out to take the key card and his licence. He wanted to call the bloke a wanker, he wanted to nut him, but he didn't want to be remembered and didn't want the filth showing up.

He nodded and strode away towards the stairs.

Chapter 39

Rose began to cry when she saw tears in Graham's eyes. She reached out and touched his face.

"It's alright, love. You can tell me all about it and then we'll decide what to do. People our age, we have stuff in the past. It doesn't matter. If you'd been married before me then it wouldn't have been a surprise that you had a daughter. I know what's upsetting you."

"No, you only think you do."

"Yes, I do. You think I'll be upset because we had so much trouble getting pregnant. Obviously if it is true that, whoever your daughter's mother is, got pregnant after just one quick bonk, then I might start to feel that it's me. My fault. You're obviously the sort who only has to shake his underpants at someone to get them pregnant, so it must have been me."

She smiled at him and he couldn't help but think she looked smug. She was being so very understanding and generous and loving it.

"None of it matters. It really doesn't. They didn't find anything actually wrong with either of us. It was just one of those things. Of course, you're older now, than you were then, I mean. So…"

She shrugged, the obvious inference that his fertility had declined because of his age. He fought back against the anger that was rising. Then she took his hand and lay it on her stomach.

"It's all fine. We've got this baby now and nothing from your past matters. We just have to look to the future. It will all be okay. Hey, maybe this girl will be a babysitter."

He pushed away from her, stood and moved to sit on the edge of the settee. "You don't understand, Rose. You really don't."

"Okay, tell me then."

He took a deep breath blowing the air out noisily through his nostrils. Why was he angry with her? She was being her lovely, kind self.

"Okay. I do know this woman's name. Of course, I do. She was called Vera Sharp. She was quite a bit older than me and she was a bit of a skank and she used to drink in The Rocket – actually, she used to drink all over the place. I think she was a druggie, but not bad. She had a job, and a flat and I'm probably making her sound much worse than she was."

"I can see why you didn't want to be with her."

"She didn't want to be with anyone."

"So, was she on the game?"

This could be a get-out for him. If he said yes, then it would explain everything. Of course, he wouldn't want to have anything to do with the child of a prostitute. It might not even be his. She had thrown him a lifeline.

"Women like that, living like that – who knows really?" he said.

"But you, did you pay her?"

"No."

She was nonplussed for a moment. The thought of admitting that he had ever paid for sex was horrible to him. Then, of course, the truth was even more ugly.

"So, you were drunk – she took advantage of you? An older woman, that happens. Was it something like that? I can see how that would be embarrassing, for a man. You have to make me understand. Honestly, you are making this much worse. Why don't you just out with it? Then you'll feel much better."

"I'd had too much to drink. It was New Year and we were all a bit mad."

"Okay, see that's not so bad. You made a mistake. I wonder why she didn't let you know though. I mean, was she so much of a slut that she didn't even know whose it was?"

"I don't think so, you've probably got the wrong idea."

"Okay, so why did she not let you know then?"

"She moved away."

"Where to?"

"I've no bloody idea, have I?"

"It's odd though, I mean, you'd have thought she'd have wanted help, wanted you to step up. You would have done, wouldn't you? I know you would. You're a decent bloke."

It was too much. She was so far off the mark and being so *understanding*, that the guilt wouldn't let him go on.

"She moved away because she couldn't stand the harassment she was getting," he said.

"Oh, what for? I mean if nobody knew she was pregnant, why was she getting harassed? Doesn't make sense."

"Tell you what, Rose. Just let it drop, yeah. I've made a complete prat of myself and I feel bad enough but you've no idea. You've no idea and I can't tell you, so just let it drop. I'll sort it."

He saw her change, the reasonable, understanding wife dropped away and the truth pushed forward.

"I don't think so. I don't think I want you spending more of my hard-earned money, spoiling my future for the kid of some skank from your past. If she moved away and you didn't know she was pregnant then chances are this is not even your daughter, so we are not spending any more. End of."

Oh, she looked so righteous, so pleased with herself. He had never realised how much it annoyed him, this facet of her personality, the know-all, the boss.

"She moved away because everyone was saying she was a whore, everyone was saying she had asked for it, everything."

"Asked for what?"

There was a long space between them. They both knew by some 'other' sense that life was about to change, it was in the air.

"I raped her, okay. I was drunk, I was stupid, and she was the bike that everyone already had a ride on. So, I took what I wanted. Are you happy now?"

Chapter 40

Rose had stormed away and left Graham in the darkening living room. He poured a drink but, in the end, didn't want it. His wife was moving about upstairs, in the bathroom, back and forth across the landing, and then the bedroom door closed with a quiet click. He trudged up to the landing and pulled a blanket and pillow out of the airing cupboard, went back, and lay on the settee staring at the cracks in the ceiling.

It was about two in the morning when Rose came down and though his eyes were closed, he felt the movement as she sat beside him.

"We have to sort this, Graham. I can't get my head around it. When you say you raped her? What do you mean? Really, do you mean she was drunk, and you took advantage? That's terrible, of course, but you were younger, it happens."

He turned his head on the pillow to look at her. It was time to get it over with. She'd leave him, sure to and he'd probably hardly ever see this kid. In truth he wasn't really sure how much that bothered him. It wasn't real yet and if she'd gone before it was born – so be it, he'd been there, done that, not that he knew it at the time.

"I had her in a back alley. She seemed as though she was up for it at first, and then she changed her mind. I was already well on the way and didn't want to stop, couldn't stop, and so I just went right ahead and forced her to let me screw her. Okay?"

"No, of course it's not okay. But at least I know now."

"And does that make you feel better, Rose? Does it?"

"No, it doesn't but at least now I know there's nothing worse. What happened after that. Were you in court?"

"No. She reported me, the police took me in 'for a chat'. But it didn't go very far. She dropped the charges pretty quickly. The cops all knew her, drunk and disorderly, causing trouble. The newspapers got a hold of it, there's always reporters nosing around. They never took it seriously. I was 'a nice lad'. A college student. My dad was a councillor. He knew the people to talk to so it would all go away. I never knew the details of how he did that, he just told me it was all 'taken care of'. Christ I was actually a choirboy so of course nobody believed her. After that she had so much harassment from everyone, the people that knew us both, the blokes in the pub, the women that disapproved of her. It wasn't like it is now. God, it's not that long ago, just over twenty years, but it was so different. Plus, I didn't hurt her, not physically. I didn't beat her up or anything. I made her have sex and for a long time I kidded myself that I hadn't done anything wrong. It was only a quick screw and she'd done it with plenty of others. Once she had gone it all died down and was forgotten about. Now though, now that it's in the media all the time, now that women talk about it more – now, I see that I was a swine. I was a criminal and I should have been punished. My name was protected. I was never charged, I brazened it out and nobody took her seriously. I see now, though, what she did. She moved away because she was pregnant, didn't she?

"When that bloke told me about the girl who believed she was my daughter, I was terrified. If it came out, now, when sex crimes are all over the news, and the papers and everywhere – if it came out now, I'd be crucified, wouldn't I? Forget my promotion to the board, forget the Masons. I expect I'd lose my job. Now there's DNA isn't there. If she proved it, who knows what could happen. So, when he said he'd make it go away, I jumped at the chance."

"And has he, do you think?"

"Has he what?"

"Made it all go away?"

"Oh yes. He's done that." He couldn't tell her. He just couldn't tell her.

"And if you pay him the rest of the money, do you think that will be the end of it?"

Rose was speaking low and quiet. He'd expected tears, shouting, banging doors, but there was just this low murmur.

"I think he will. I've told him there's no more."

"Okay. In that case, you see him and tell him this is it and make him believe you."

"But, what about us? What about you and the baby?"

"That's the whole point. I'll have to get over it, won't I? I'll not have this baby growing up with no dad or worse growing up with a dad who is known as a sex fiend. So, we'll get through this. It'll never be the same – never – but we'll just have to make it work. I don't ever want to see her though, this girl. There must be no contact, she can't be part of our lives."

"She won't be. I can promise you that one hundred per cent, she won't be."

Chapter 41

Terry turned up on Monday morning looking worse for wear and still stinking a bit of alcohol.

"Good night, was it?" Jordan asked.

"Yeah. Turned into quite a session in the end. But I'm okay now, boss. Ready to go. Least I will be when I've finished this coffee."

"Bring it with you. We've got our warrants and I want to have a look at Ben's room before his mother has a chance to speak to him. Though I do know that we might be too late. Detective Constable Searle has already left for the Wirral to have a look through the papers there and bring back copies. She's taken Beverly Powell with her. She might be a bit uptight but she's good with documentation."

Once they were in the car Terry drained his takeaway mug and put it in the passenger footwell with a promise to move it later. Jordan offered him a packet of mints.

"I know we earn our time off, Detective Constable, but you need to think about forward planning and sometimes just exercise a bit of control."

"Yes, boss. I hear you. Sorry."

Jordan smiled and nodded. "How's your mum?"

"She's fine, thanks."

"Over the shock, is she?"

"Yeah. She's tough, the old lady."

"Did she lose much?" Jordan asked.

"Nah. She got most of it back?"

"How come?"

There was a loaded silence as Terry realised that he'd been backed into a corner.

"Our Steve found her stuff. Bloody lucky that."

Jordan glanced across the car and watched colour flood Terry's cheeks.

"As I said the other day, Terry, you really need to be careful. It doesn't take much for things to go horribly wrong."

Terry turned away to look out of the window, but Jordan noticed him picking at the scabs on his knuckles. Best to let it drop and just hope the message had been received.

* * *

They knocked hard on the front door of the little house in Bootle. Ben's mum appeared after a couple of minutes, bleary-eyed, blinking in the light.

"What the hell is this? It's the middle of the bloody night."

Jordan lifted his arm to look at his watch. "It's after seven, Mrs Harwood. We did tell you we'd be coming back."

"You didn't say you'd be getting decent folk out of their beds."

As she spoke, she dragged a hand through her dishevelled hair, finger ends digging into her scalp.

Jordan held up the warrant and they moved forward. They didn't touch the woman, but she had no option but to move out of their way. She scurried along the narrow hallway in front of them and stood at the foot of the stairs.

"Our Doris is still in bed."

"Could you go and ask her to come out of the room, please?" Jordan said. "In the meantime, we'll just go and have a look in the living room."

"No, you bloody won't. This paper says you are looking at our Ben's stuff."

"And there is nothing of his in there?"

"No, there isn't. He doesn't go in there much. He stays in his room. That's where he works, where he watches telly and all that. That's mine in there."

"It won't take us long then, will it?" Terry pushed open the door as he spoke.

"Bloody police harassment this is. I'll be telling the papers. You can't come in here like this, pushing people about. He hasn't done anything. I've told you that."

Doris appeared on the landing, she was wrapped in a fluffy dressing gown, a pink cap covering her curlers.

"What the hell is going on, Jean? It's like a loony bin in here?"

"I'm sorry, love, these gobshites are throwing their weight around, scaring defenceless women in their own homes. I'll be reporting this, don't you worry."

"Mrs Harwood, we have no intention of frightening you. There's no need at all for this to be anything more than just a look at Ben's things. It is a very serious crime and we would like to eliminate him from our enquiries."

"They should have sent a woman. Should have sent somebody... local."

Jordan ignored the latent racism. He'd heard it all before.

At the sound of Terry clattering around in her living room the woman stalked across the space and Jordan ran up the stairs, past the confused sister on the landing and into the room at the front of the house.

It wasn't a large room but there was a range of built-in wardrobes lining the longest wall. A single bed took up the space in a narrow alcove and then around the corner and under the window was a desk served by a bank of electrical

155

sockets. On the desktop was a nylon bag, the top gaping open disclosing bottles and tubes. There was a hairbrush and comb and a pair of tights in a bundle at the end. A tiny plastic alarm clock ticked happily away in the middle. There was no computer, no monitor, keyboard, earphones, nothing that they would have expected to find in the room of someone who made his living working on the internet.

Jordan was aware that Doris had come to stand in the doorway. He turned and smiled at her. She did not smile back.

"Where is Ben's stuff?"

"Don't know what you mean. That's all mine so you can keep your hands off it."

"I haven't touched it, ma'am. I need to see the things belonging to your nephew. Have you stored them away somewhere?"

"Not my business. Our Jean has made me very welcome. She's cleared out this room for me."

Jordan opened the wardrobe nearest to him. Jeans and hoodies hung neatly inside. He glanced at Doris.

"Of course she couldn't move all of his stuff. It has to go somewhere," she said.

There was a set of drawers under the hanging space and Jordan pulled it open and lifted out the top drawer. He tipped the contents onto the unmade bed.

"Jean, this bloke's ransacking our Ben's stuff."

There was huffing and tutting and at one stage Jean Harwood began folding the clothes and piling them onto the dresser.

"It's disgusting. Treating people like this. Innocent people."

There was no point arguing, there was no point hoping for sense to prevail, so Terry and Jordan worked through the drawers, the cupboard and even the basket of dirty linen. There were a few dirty clothes and some old shoes, a few magazines, and some older computer games in boxes. No game consoles, no joystick or mini steering wheel. A scratched mobile phone was stuffed into the back of one of the drawers. Terry pulled it out with his gloved fingers and pressed the button.

"Flat," he said. "Is this Ben's?"

"Don't know. It's not mine. It's probably one of his old ones." Terry slipped the phone into an evidence bag, sealed and labelled it and set it to one side. "Can't see a charger for it," he said.

"Where are all Ben's other electronics?" Jordan asked.

The woman shrugged and sniffed.

"We'll have to go through your room, your kitchen, wherever, unless you tell us."

"I don't know. He might have taken some things with him. He might have put things in his lock-up. He doesn't like me touching his stuff. He's got screens, speakers and microphones. But I don't touch it, so he's probably put it somewhere out of the way."

"Where is his lock-up?"

By this time, she knew she was beaten, they were determined, and the best thing would be to get them out of the house as quickly as possible. She gave them instructions on how to get to the storage unit.

"Ben's phone number?" Jordan said.

"Don't know it; how can I be expected to remember those long numbers?"

"Could you get it from your phone?"

"No. I don't think it's on there."

"That's very difficult to believe."

"Difficult or not, I'm telling you."

"We can get another warrant. One to examine your things."

"You do that, lad. But now, if you've finished wrecking my house, just bugger off."

Jordan decided that they might as well give it up. Ben had obviously moved more stuff than would have been reasonable for someone away on a business trip, but they weren't going to get anywhere with the mother, and they were wasting time.

"Right, Terry, let's go round to the lock-up. Have you got a key, love, or do you want us to just break in?"

She handed over the ring of keys with a snarl and they left the two women to chunter and complain as they refolded the clothes and put them away.

"Bloody waste of time," Terry said.

"Yeah, it might seem so, but I think something's going on. You don't take spare monitors and what have you for just for a week or two on a course, no matter who is going to be using your room. His mother said that she doesn't touch his stuff and yet the aunty told us she'd moved them. It doesn't add up. I reckon he's gone for longer than that. Unless of course it is all stowed in the lock-up. But would you leave electronics in that sort of environment? We'll go and see of course but I'm not holding out much hope."

Chapter 42

The lock-up was in a row of other similar little garages. Concrete-block walls, flat rooves and metal roller shutter doors. The hefty padlock was fairly new, and the key slid in smoothly.

"Shoulda used a combination lock," Terry said.

"Lucky for us that he didn't. Come on give us a hand."

They rolled open the shutter. It was tidy inside. No car, but they hadn't expected there to be. There was a racing bike propped against one wall, a metal tool cabinet, and some plastic boxes. Terry moved forward but Jordan held out a hand.

"D'ya know what, I reckon we should get SOCO up here."

"Why?" Terry asked.

"Gut feeling, not much more to be honest but I'm sticking with it. Anyway, it'll give you another chance to ogle Sergeant Bailey."

"I'll get on to them." They laughed as he dialled.

While Terry made the call, Jordan paced around the small yard. All the other units were locked, some with padlocks, some with heavy duty bolts and hasps. There were oil stains, and puddles here and there where the concrete was uneven and a tap at the far end with a grate underneath.

"They can't get here until this affie. Apparently, there's a job down by the Pier Head and they're helping out. A body in one of the hotels."

"Who's handling it?"

"Dunno, boss. Not us obviously. Unless we've missed the calls. They both clicked through the call list on their phones.

"Nothing here," Jordan said.

"No, nor me. It'll be city centre I should think. Anyway, I've logged the call and they said they'll send someone soon as."

"Good enough."

"Do you still not want to have a look inside. Under the circumstances," Terry said.

"Go on then. Suits and boots in my car. Take plenty of pictures and be careful. Don't disturb things too much."

There wasn't very much to disturb. The bike was just what it looked like, though they would have samples of the dirt taken from the tyres, just in case it told them anything. The toolbox was surprisingly carefully looked after. Everything in it was clean, no rust and the spare screws and washers that there were had been stored in plastic tubs. The wooden cupboard against the wall was old and battered but the doors swung open easily. On the top shelf were some pieces of towelling, obviously for mopping up and cleaning. A pair of old trainers which Jordan slid into an evidence bag and fairly predictably, some porn magazines. They were in a plastic envelope and those were bagged and tagged.

On the bottom shelf at the back was a bulky Tesco carrier and Jordan pulled it forward. Using his gloved fingertips, he opened the top.

"Terry, come and get a picture of this, will you?"

"What have you got, boss?"

"If I'm lucky I may have a weapon. Look, the glass is broken. The metal is dented. I'm not taking it out of this bag. Let's leave it for lovely Sergeant Bailey. It looks well dodgy. Why would he stick it in the back of the cupboard. If it's broken to the extent that it doesn't work, surely he'd just chuck it."

"It's clean though, from what we can see."

"Right. Right." As he spoke Jordan turned around, leaving the torch in the cupboard and rushed to the door. "In the back of my car there's a sheet of plastic. Fetch it would you."

While Terry brought the blue sheet, Jordan ran to the entrance of the little yard where he'd noticed a pile of concrete blocks.

"Right, spread it over that grate, we can hold it down with these."

"What's your thinking, boss?"

"If that is our weapon it must have been covered in blood and brain matter. He might have washed it off here. There hasn't been a lot of rain in the last few days. Sergeant Bailey might be able to find some of her 'nice juicy' evidence. I think we'll just hang on here until she can join us. I don't want us screwing things up now that it looks as though we might be moving forward. I've got a couple of cans of Coke in my car, maybe even a bar of chocolate. Come on."

Chapter 43

Groups of disgruntled guests had been ushered into the bar and dining area of the hotel. Waiters were doing the rounds with drinks and biscuits, but the police were hassled by frustrated and impatient punters. They didn't want to wait around, didn't want to give their details. They had shopping to do, trips to take and meetings to attend. They gawped when the crime scene tape was stretched across the corridor and the hubbub increased when the white-suited technicians drew up outside and the crew carted in their boxes and bags.

Sergeant Vivienne Bailey scanned the restaurant area.

"Bloody Norah. Had to be busy didn't it," she grumbled to the SIO who had come to stand beside her.

"Yeah, I know. We'll get through them as quick as we can, starting with the ones on the same floor as our body. The medical examiner is up there already. Phil Grant. I think you know her."

"Yeah, good. No doubt that it was a suspicious death, I suppose?"

He shook his head.

"Not unless the bloke was a contortionist. Knife wounds in his back, it's a bit nasty to be honest. They're going to have trouble getting the stains out of the carpet."

Black humour told her that it was going to be a messy scene. She did like a messy scene. She rubbed her hands together.

"I'll get on then, leave you to the punters. Come on, guys." She led her team of technicians across the hallway and into the lifts.

There was blood in the corridor, just a spatter by the door, but a trail of it across the room. The body was splayed half on and half off the bed, the head turned towards the window. Blood had pooled on the pale duvet and run to drip onto the carpet.

Bailey turned to the technician beside her.

"Carpet's a goner, I reckon."

She waited until the safe route had been established with plastic mats and then moved forward to look at the corpse. The medical examiner walked in front of her, dictating first impressions into her recording unit. She nodded as she raised a hand.

"Hello, Viv. You okay?"

"I am thanks. Better than this bloke at least." The conversation was muffled by masks, but it was unimportant, just a social nicety, keeping things normal.

She leaned forward to get a better view of the pale face, eyes staring towards the window. She nodded, murmured to herself.

"Oh, right."

It was tricky removing her phone from underneath the paper suit but she dragged it out with her fingertips.

"Jordan, I think you should get down here. I'm in a hotel in the city centre, I'll send you directions. There's someone here I reckon you want to meet. Not going to be able to tell you much, not until the medical examiner has had a go at him."

She didn't say any more, just clicked off the phone and joined her team in their routine.

* * *

Jordan tried ringing back, but the call went straight to the answering system. He'd have to trust that the SOCO sergeant wouldn't be wasting his time. She knew what he was working on and she wasn't stupid. He'd just have to get down there and see what was what.

"Right, sorry, Terry. I'm going to have to leave you here. Secure that unit, and don't let anyone use the tap. I don't know what's going on, but the lovely Vivienne has called, and I really think this is important. I'll either come back to pick you up or send a car. Don't think it's going to rain, but you can borrow my anorak if you like."

"No, you're alright, boss, thanks though. Let me know what's going on, yeah."

"I will. Here, have the rest of the chocolate."

Chapter 44

The drive from Bootle to the city centre was only fifteen minutes. But it felt longer – Jordan was intrigued and impatient. When he saw the official cars and the crowds gathering outside the hotel, his confusion grew.

"Who is SIO?" He had flipped open his warrant card at the door and was ushered through by a uniformed constable.

"DI Grice. He's over in the restaurant, sir."

Jordan recognised Andy Grice. He'd met him now and again at functions and lectures, so he didn't need to introduce himself.

"What's brought you down here, Jordan?"

"Call from Sergeant Bailey. Not sure why, to be honest, she was a bit… vague."

"Ha. Yes, that's Viv for you. She's upstairs, second floor, follow the route. There are suits and whatnot over there." He pointed to a couple of cardboard boxes at the doorway. "Sorry but you can't use the lift, we've roped it off until SOCO have had a chance to process it."

"Not a problem."

"You won't be saying that in another ten years and with a couple of extra stone to cart around. He slapped at the bulge in the front of his uniform. Hold on, I'll let the crime scene manager know you're on the way up. It's pretty gory up there."

There was a muttered back and forth on the Airwave system and then DI Grice waved a hand towards the stairs as he went off to intervene in a stand-off between the constable on door duty and a family wanting lunch.

A couple of the technicians glanced up at Jordan when he appeared at the hotel room door. He could see Phil Grant in conversation with Vivienne Bailey. He was waved into the room and used the stepping plates to reach the blood-stained bed.

Vivienne Bailey turned as he arrived and performed an over-the-top pantomime bow and flourish with her arms.

"I think you might have been looking for this bloke."

Jordan was literally speechless. If he had been forced to hazard a guess, finding Ben Harwood on a gore-splattered bed in a city centre hotel would never have come into his mind. He leaned over the corpse, glancing up at the two women who were watching him in silence. He wagged his phone in the air – the crime scene manager nodded at him. It probably hadn't been necessary, but Jordan liked to stick to the rules wherever possible. He took a couple of pictures, straightened up and in the absence of anything else coming to mind he just said, "Well, bugger me."

"If you like, but I'm a bit busy right now," Viv Bailey said. The two women tittered together. "Are you blushing, Inspector? Hard to tell."

Coming from another source this could have been racist but when Sergeant Bailey said it, it was impossible to take offence.

"Thank you, Sergeant."

Jordan was grinning back at them. From behind the mask, all they could make out was the glint in his eyes. Phil Grant had to remind herself that it was commonly known he was very married and a new dad. She turned away.

"This might cause some logistical problems for you. But that's your concern. Just let me know who needs a copy of my report. I'll get to the examination by tomorrow afternoon with luck. Oh yes, for the avoidance of doubt. Life is extinct. Probably all to do with the holes in his back."

Jordan left them to it and walked back into the hallway. He sent the images to Terry Denn waiting in Bootle telling him he'd be relieved by a uniformed officer and to get back as soon as he could. Then another copy to Beverly Powell for the incident room board.

Hey – Look what we've found.

Okay it was a little unprofessional but spending time in the company of the two women had lifted his mood.

Chapter 45

Rose pulled the curtains closed and poured them both a glass of whisky. Graham took his but frowned when he saw her take a sip.

"Oh, for god's sake, Graham, it's one tiny drink and I think I need it. The stress is probably doing more harm to this baby than a tot of whisky will."

He nodded and took a gulp from his glass.

"Tell me then, how was it? I've been on pins all day, thinking about it, watching the clock. I wanted to call you, but it might have been just the wrong time. I've yelled at the secretary, then I had to apologise. I told her it was hormones and she gave me a big hug. I felt really mean. It was horrible. I had to have a meeting with Gerald about how we manage things as I get bigger. I'll carry on with my classes, but I can't do the weight training and probably not the swimming, once I look ridiculous in a swimsuit. They are going to get in a second personal trainer to help out. I've got all this going on and you and this blackmailer filling my mind at the same time. It's crap, I can't do it. In the end I flexed off. I had time owing anyway and Monday's usually quiet."

Graham sighed and pulled down the corners of his mouth.

"I'm sorry, love. Look there'll be time to plan all your work and what have you when this is sorted. There's no rush. As long as you're being careful at the gym. And they do take care of you, don't they?"

"Yes, they do. But just tell me, how did it go. With this arse?"

"I don't know, Rose. What do I compare it with? It was okay I suppose – for paying off a blackmailer."

"So where did you meet him?"

"Okay, he messaged me mid-morning. I met him by the Beatles statue at the Pier Head. I suppose he wanted somewhere pretty public. To be honest I was okay with that as well, and it was handy for the office. Anyway, he was just ordinary. Younger than I expected. He was a bit of a yob, I reckon. Jeans, a hoody, trainers. He had a hat pulled down over his forehead and I don't really think I got a clear look at his face."

"But that was him, definitely?"

"How do you mean?"

"What I mean is, how did you know it was him? How could you be sure? You were one hundred per cent sure, weren't you? I mean it wasn't somebody he got to do it for him?"

"I didn't think of that. It was all a bit stupid really, like something out of a naff film. He was carrying a copy of the Echo and I had to have my briefcase and put it beside my feet while I was standing by John Lennon. He made me tell him what I was wearing, on the phone, you know. I think he was partly just being daft and partly trying to ridicule me. There were people taking pictures and they kept asking me to move. In the end he came up and he just said 'Over here' so I followed him, and he held his hand out. I gave him the envelope with the money, and he nodded and walked away. It wasn't like some sort of spy movie or something. I just felt ridiculous."

"But it was him? I mean, how sure are you that it wasn't somebody he'd sent?" Rose asked again.

"I don't know. Why would he do that, why involve someone else? I think it was him, he didn't say much so I couldn't tell from his voice. It's possible, I suppose. But what else could I do except give it to him?"

"What happened then?"

"Nothing, it was weird really. I just went back to the office. I had meetings and then I came home.

"So, that's it then? It's over?"

"Do you think so? I'd love to agree, Rose, maybe though, eh? Once I've given him the rest of it. Maybe it is all over now."

"And that girl. How can we be sure she's not going to turn up?" Rose said.

"No, she won't. She's not going to turn up, you don't need to worry about that, one hundred per cent."

"I bloody hope not. Anyway, we need to calm down. We need to find a way to put all this behind us. I'm not kidding you, Graham, you've let me down. You really have."

"Yes, I know. Do you think there's a way forward for us?"

She leaned and pulled his hand towards her belly, smiled at him.

"There has to be. We'll do up the box room, like you say. We'll tell people the move is too much at the moment and then in a year or so we can go back to our plans. There'll still be time to get 'Blob' into a good school."

"Blob?"

"Yeah, I think of it as Blob at the moment. Until we decide whether we want to know the sex."

"Blob. Okay." He raised his glass.

Chapter 46

Jordan was relieved that he wouldn't be the one taking the bad news to Jean Harwood. The job fell to Andy Grice as current SIO of the killing in the city centre. He couldn't help but imagine the scene. They all hated it, delivering the 'hard word', and he was glad that the woman had her sister there to be with her. She had loved her son. She had been proud of him. Though it was obvious that bad news had been coming her way soon, he never imagined it would be this.

He spent a restless evening and night. Penny asked him repeatedly what was on his mind, but he tried to keep the horror away from his family.

"Just work stuff, love. It's nothing to bother about. I'll sort it."

He was desperate to sort out who would take the case and could do nothing until his meeting with the DCI next day. Andy Grice was an experienced and capable officer. He'd be perfectly able to handle it, but Jordan didn't want him to. There was no doubt in his mind that the two killings were linked. They had to be. Everyone could see that. Surely. Beverly Powell, when she had posted the gory images on the board at the station, had placed the two victims side by side, linked with a red line. They had talked it around and around until after nine in the evening but with no technical reports and no decision about protocol it had all been edgy and difficult. Richard Cross had been unavailable, though Jordan had left several messages on his phone. At the end of the day, this new killing wasn't on his patch and that meant he would be reading about it in the reports in the morning. It was torment.

* * *

There was a chorus of greetings as he arrived in work, everyone looking to him for news he didn't have. He shook his head.

"Did you send that phone from Bootle to the Digital Forensics Lab?" he asked Terry Denn.

"Yes, I took it down myself as soon as we got back yesterday. I don't think it's going to be any use, though."

"Why's that?"

"The tech bloke knew straight away that there was no battery in it. Too light, he said. He opened it up while I was there and sure enough, just a space where the battery should be. He reckons it was long past being used. Anyway, they are going to get it fired up and see what's on it. I asked him to get a shift on. Promised him a bottle of something. Mind you, didn't say what. Could be milk." There was a quiet round of laughter.

"Okay, thanks. Keep on at them, will you? I have a meeting this morning to decide the way forward and I'm determined that we'll get this case. I know we're thin on the ground and you've all been working hard but he's ours. Yeah?"

They were behind him one hundred per cent and he was impatient to have the meeting with Richard Cross, get everything official.

* * *

DCI Cross was disgruntled.

"All getting a bit complicated, Jordan. We were just helping out Campbell in Waterloo and now we've got ourselves involved with the chaps down St Anne Street."

"I think, sir, that we should take it from them. I don't think there is any need for them to be involved. I know DI Grice is a capable officer, but I was already looking for Ben Harwood."

"Shame you didn't find him before he got himself stabbed then, isn't it?"

There was no reasonable answer to the outburst. Jordan nodded and hoped it would be enough.

"As you can imagine their brass is happy to palm it off on us. Not Andy Grice of course, he's champing at the bit, but you can have it. Don't let me down, Jordan. I don't want any more bloody corpses, no more death. Sort this out."

"Yes, sir. Thank you."

The team could tell by his face that they'd won and there was a murmur of approval as he walked to the board in the corner.

"Right. A quick recap and then we need to start making some decent progress. Where's DC Denn?"

"Been called down to the Digital Forensics Lab, sir. He said something on the phone about 'two bloody bottles' just before he left."

"Okay. I've got to get down to the hotel. Got a walkthrough of the scene with DI Grice and SOCO ready for them to hand it over."

"Oh, is that with Sergeant Bailey?" He hadn't heard Terry Denn come back into the office.

"Yes, it is. Why?"

"Just wondered if you wanted me to come."

There were a few laughs around the room and then Rosalind Searle spoke up.

"You do know you're wasting your time there don't you, Terry?"

"Why? Is she with someone?"

"You could say. She lives with her partner."

"Aw. Who is he? I could work on him, get rid." They knew he was joking but then the room erupted as Rosalind stood from the desk and went to get a bottle of water from the machine in the corridor. "I believe her name is Rebecca."

Terry waited for a couple of minutes. He didn't blush exactly, but Jordan had never seen him look so sheepish.

"Yeah, I knew that," he said. "Of course I did, just feels like a bit of a waste that's all. Perhaps I could change her mind." There was a sudden hush. A tense hiatus. A couple of the women went back to their computers, eyes down.

Jordan clapped his hands together.

"Okay, so what did you need to go dashing off to the technicians for?"

"Oh yeah." Terry grabbed at the lifeline. He knew he'd slipped and the sooner they moved on the better. He needed to impress them now and fortunately he had the means. "Let me just plug this in." He held up a memory stick. "Could someone turn on the big monitor?"

The image was shocking, and a couple of the civilians turned away but there were gasps and expletives as Beatrice's battered body filled the screen.

"So, this was the only picture on that phone. There is other stuff, contacts, messages and what have you, but if there were other pictures, which would be likely, then they have been deleted. The bloke that is working on it has the number and they are tracing the owner now. Going to contact us, soon as."

"But we know the owner, don't we?" Rosalind Searle said.

"Well, we know that the phone was in Ben's house. But here's the thing. The metadata shows that this picture wasn't taken with this phone."

"So, what does that mean?" Searle asked.

"To be honest, I'm not absolutely sure. But it seems to indicate that there could have been someone else involved. At the very least it shows that there was another phone. Why someone would do that? Your guess is as good as mine," Terry said.

"Did they give you any idea how long before they trace the owner?"

Terry's phone chimed, he glanced at the screen. "That's them now."

Chapter 47

Terry Denn drove them into Liverpool.

"I have to do this walkthrough. In the meantime, I want you to go to the post-mortem examination. It's nearly half eleven now. Pick me up afterwards. Then we need to go and have a conversation with the owner of that phone. I also want you to call Sergeant Bailey and make sure she's going to go and process Harwood's lock-up. We've had a uniformed officer stationed there since yesterday and it's time to close that down."

"Sir."

Jordan knew that Terry would have done anything to get out of calling Vivienne Bailey. There was no doubt that the story of his embarrassment in the incident room would have got back to her. It was better done quickly and though she was quirky and different, Jordan knew she was also professional, and kind. She might make him squirm a bit, but it wouldn't do him any harm.

"I think it might be a good idea for DC Searle to come with me to talk to Mrs Harwood later. No reflection on you at all, Terry, but a woman in this situation might be a good idea and I am aware that we could have used her more.

Chapter 48

"Morning, Jordan." Andy Grice seemed perfectly happy to be handing over the case.

"You okay with… everything, Andy?" Jordan asked.

"Yeah. Let's face it, at best this would have been a collaboration, with you already looking for him. I won't lie, a high-profile case wouldn't have done me any harm, but I'd rather work on my own. Anyway, if we can help just let us know. We can go round the scene now if you like. I've already sent the witness statements over to your place. Not much to tell you to be honest. The housekeeper noticed the spatter on the carpet, thought it was food spillage at first but then when she looked through the door – mayhem. The bloke checked in as normal, almost, he paid cash and didn't want to show ID but apart from that, nothing. Nobody remembers seeing him in the bar or the dining area and to be honest people are in and out of the place all day long. It's not like there's a porter or anything so it's not a surprise that nobody noticed him."

"Did you get his belongings or was the room cleared out?"

"It looks, on the face of it, that we recovered everything. No sign of robbery. We found a couple of bags of clothes, his laptop, phone and what have you, even computer gaming equipment, and his wallet. It's all been taken bagged and tagged, and I've let them know that the reports are to come to you." He pulled out his notebook. "Couple of things that might be of help right away. He had a ticket for the boat to Belfast for last night and there was a set of keys, car and house door. We haven't been able to trace a vehicle yet. The hotel doesn't have its own car park. We've been looking at the CCTV but no joy up to now. It's busy. Have you any idea what sort of a vehicle he has? There is a licence number on the ferry ticket but it doesn't check out with DVLA, so I reckon he fudged that."

"As far as we know he'd have been in a white van. A Ford Connect. That's what he had on some CCTV that we viewed. What plate number did you have?"

They peered together at the page, and Jordan took out his phone to check his own records.

"Ah, so he's just transposed a couple of numbers. Okay, we can work with that. I can get some uniforms to have a look around for a van with either reg," Jordan said.

"Listen, we had already started so why don't I let you know when we find it?"

"That's decent of you. Cheers. I owe you one," Jordan said.

"Now that we know just what we're looking for it shouldn't take long. Tell you what, you arrange for transport for it and as soon as I have a location I'll give you a bell. Now, if there's nothing else I've got a couple of violent robberies to work on, so we'll go up to the room then I'll have to shoot."

"I really appreciate your help, Andy."

"Hey, there'll come a time when I need something from you. You wait and see. It makes the world go round. Our sleazy, nasty little bit of it anyway."

* * *

After he collected Terry it didn't take Jordan long to fill him in on his meeting with Grice, and the rest of the drive was spent giving Terry a rundown of the post-mortem examination.

"Death due to blood loss caused by several stab wounds to the back and neck, nasty damage to the spinal cord so he probably wouldn't have ever recovered in any real sense. A long knife with a sharp point. Dr Grant thought just an ordinary chef's knife. The sort you find in most kitchens these days. Would need to be someone pretty fit but there were no defence wounds, so it looks as though he turned his back on his attacker and then was taken by surprise."

"So, he either knew his attacker or didn't feel threatened."

"Seems right. Nothing else surprising, evidence of occasional drug use but not alarming. Last meal was a burger and chips and a fizzy drink. Not super fit, about average really. Probably didn't work out but was just reasonably active. That's pretty good for someone who works with computers apparently. The long hours behind a desk can play havoc with fitness levels according to the doctor."

"Not much help really. Let's hope we can get more from his computer and phone," Jordan said.

"Bev Powell asked me to let you know that she might have found something in the paperwork they brought back from the company. She wouldn't tell me what it was. Wants to talk to you directly."

"Okay. I think I need to have a word there, get her working as part of the team. She is very keen to shine alone, but it's not helpful."

"Aye well. Wants to be teacher's pet, I reckon."

"Hmm. Okay this is us. What's this bloke's name?"

"Ronnie O'Grady. Don't have much information. I've seen some of his texts. He's not working, likes a drink with his mates, lives with his sister. Nothing on our system

about him. No activity on the phone from the day after
Beatrice was killed."

Chapter 49

"Yeah that looks like mine." Ronnie O'Grady looked at the phone in its plastic evidence bag. "That scratch on the screen, I remember that. Some arsehole nicked it from me at the pub."

"You didn't report it?" Jordan asked.

"A cheap pay-as-you-go with ten quid credit. What do you think? Nah. I called Tesco, got them to transfer my number. My sister bought me a new one. It's my birthday next week."

"Did you know him? The bloke who took it?"

"Nope, never seen him before. An effin' wanker. I reckon he picked a fight deliberately. How sad is that? Just for a scuzzy little handset."

"Do you know this man?" Jordan held out a copy of the photograph of Ben Harwood.

"That's him. That's the sad bastard."

"We have alerts out, on the internet and so on asking for information. Did you not see them?"

"On the telly, were they?"

"No. Not on the television."

The youth shrugged his shoulders.

"Do you think I waste my time on Facebook? How old do you think I am? What's he done anyway?"

"He's got himself killed." Terry didn't mince his words.

"Shit." As he spoke O'Grady held up his hands. "Don't look at me. I haven't done anything. It's a crap little phone. You'd better not be looking at me. I don't think I want to say anything else."

"Really, Mr O'Grady, don't panic. Ronnie, we are not suggesting you have done anything untoward. We simply want to know anything at all you can tell us about this man. We do believe that he might have been involved in a serious crime and we need to trace anyone who might have had contact with him."

"You're not looking at me?"

"No."

"Ok. As I say, we were in the pub. He picked a fight. Pretended to fall and I reckon that was when he nicked my phone."

"I'd like you to look at this image." Jordan held up the picture of Beatrice. "Do you know her?"

"No. Not my type, I like 'em with a bit more umph – know what I mean? She could be alright if she did herself up a bit, but no – never seen her before."

"Right, thank you, Mr O'Grady. I think that's all. We'll get this phone back to you in due course, but it could be a while, to be honest."

"No. Don't worry about it. I've got my new one now."

* * *

"Next to nothing from that then. Why the hell did he have this picture on a stolen phone but never did anything with it?" Jordan muttered.

He thought for a moment then looked up.

"Right, Terry, back to base. We need to regroup. See how this all fits together. It's got to but I have no idea how. I'll just ring my wife and tell her I'm probably going to be late, again."

Chapter 50

Back in the incident room, the whole team was still there. Many of them were short of things to do but yet again they didn't want to miss anything. Something had to happen soon. It had to, otherwise this was going to turn into the sort of case nobody wanted to be connected with. Surely, with this new development they must be moving forward. So, they stayed and went over things again and waited for the reports to come in on Harwood, and for the ends to start to come together.

Beverly Powell stood up as Jordan slid his tablet computer onto the desk and slung his jacket over the back of a chair. She collected her papers together and hovered in the corner of the room, staring at him, waiting.

He glanced across at her. She was like an impatient school child. He nodded.

"I believe you wanted a word?"

She waved the sheaf of printouts in the air and crossed the room.

"These are the hard copies of the records from Time Tracers. There's the stuff that Ben Harwood was working on recently. Nothing stood out there. Most of his projects were completed and the clients seemed to be happy with what they received." She put the small pile of paper aside.

"We have the contact records for the last couple of months for the whole company. I've highlighted those that were specifically Ben Harwood's and most of them correlate with the first list. Mr Lipscowe didn't want to let us have them for obvious reasons, but DC Searle convinced him that it was better to comply rather than us have them requisitioned which might include examination of the company records as a whole. She hinted at tax and whatnot."

She made yet another neat pile, squaring off the edges of the sheets. Jordan wished that she'd stop fannying about and just get on with it.

"He's a nice guy really, I think he's just a bit out of his depth. He's fairly reserved and spends his life locked in his online world looking back in time. Anyway, that's not really relevant. The thing is they have a file for tracings that are abandoned for various reasons. Customers change their minds, decide it's not worth the cost, all that sort of thing. And look, Beatrice Sharp did contact them. Ben Harwood took the job, but then he stuck it into the deleted folder with a note that the client had cancelled. There is no cancellation email. Nothing in fact other than the original request for help and then the note archiving it."

"Did Mr Lipscowe have any explanation?"

"No, quite a lot of people change their minds. Though he did find it odd that there wasn't a record of the second communication informing them that she wished to cancel, and he would have expected at least one chasing email. Not hard selling, he insisted, but just a reminder that they'd made contact. They have a system so they can try to pull people back in. Harwood hadn't followed it but Lipscowe didn't seem bothered. I don't think he runs by very strict rules."

Jordan had taken the papers and laid them on the desk to look at them.

"So, what if she didn't change her mind and Ben Harwood was doing a bit on the side? What if she didn't like what he'd found, or I suppose what if he told her he didn't want to continue with it, though that seems unlikely? I mean even if he found out something nasty it wouldn't reflect on him. In any case, it seems suspicious with hindsight of course. There is initial contact and then he bins the details and effectively cuts off all contact. Later he is seen loitering around the area on the day she dies. Too many questions, too many coincidences."

He looked up now.

"You could have given this to DC Searle, Beverly. It needs to be reported to the Digital Forensics Lab. We need to do our own search, find out whether there was any further contact. There could be emails or information on Ben's laptop. We never did find Beatrice's computer or phone. There's something definitely dodgy and they could have made a start already. They'll need to arrange access to the company computers at Time Tracers. They may even need help from Lipscowe. They should have known about this. It's important and it could have saved them time. This should all have been in hand."

"I thought you'd want to know about it, first."

"Okay, but you could have just let me know, sent a message. You told DC Denn that you'd found something, why not tell him how important it was? He hadn't a clue. You shouldn't have kept it to yourself. Right. Give this to DC Searle and ask her to come and have a word."

Beverly glared at him as she turned away, so she didn't see him shake his head and cover his face with his hands. He picked up the phone to talk to a mate in the Digital Forensics Lab trying to pull in a favour and get them working on it immediately in conjunction with the work on Ben Harwood's own machine. This was big, he could feel it. He didn't want to let Beverly Powell know how big right now. He would give her credit in due course. For now, he was irritated that she had sat on this information all day for no other reason than she wanted to give it to him personally. He was going to have to do something about her. She was becoming a liability.

He sent Rosalind Searle away with the printouts and everything they knew about timetracers.com. Now he would have to leave it to the technical people. He didn't have the skill or the knowledge to work on this himself and he would only be in their way. He called Stan Lipscowe to let him know he should expect visitors.

"But he was working remotely, all my people do. There'll be nothing here," he argued.

"We have his computer now and of course we'll be examining that, but we will need access to your own files. We may need your help to solve this. I'm sorry, sir."

"If you've got his computer why can't you just ask him?"

When Jordan explained exactly why they couldn't ask Ben Harwood, there was no more argument from Lipscowe, which was a step in the right direction.

"Anything I can do. Anything at all."

Jordan was sure that the man's voice broke as he ended the call.

The next time the phone rang it was from Andy Grice and the frustration disappeared completely.

"Jordan, we've found your van. Down here, not far from the hotel."

"Fantastic. I'll send the recovery vehicle down and SOCO'll be on their way within the hour. They were standing by."

"Oh, are you going to send Vivienne Bailey? Go on, please. That'll be a perfect end to a long shift."

Jordan laughed. He wouldn't tell him what he had just discovered about her preferences. She had obviously managed to keep her private life fairly low key and it wasn't his way to gossip. Anyway, if it brightened Andy's day to spend time with Sergeant Bailey – honestly, he owed him that.

"It's not up to me but I'll do what I can. Enjoy."

Chapter 51

Jordan had a FaceTime call to see Harry before he went to bed. The little boy was old enough to recognise his daddy's voice on the computer and reach out podgy fingers to the screen. It wasn't much, but it was better than nothing.

"How's it going?" Penny asked.

"Not sure to be honest, love. Could have made a bit of a breakthrough today but it's only going to get us so far."

Jordan didn't like sharing the more gory details of his job but Penny was grounded and calm.

"Did you see the report of the death in the city centre, the hotel?" he said.

"I did. That's not yours though is it? Not your patch?"

"No, but it's our body. It's the bloke I've been looking for."

"Oh, crap. That's not good is it?"

"No. Hasn't gone down all that well, I have to say."

"Oh, I'm sorry, Jordan. You'll sort it. You know you will."

He didn't know how to respond to such loyalty. Such belief.

"Thanks. Penny. Listen it could be another late one. I'm sorry."

"It's fine. I've got some paperwork to go through for my new job so I'm busy. I'll see you later. Do you want me to leave you something to eat?"

"No, don't bother. We sent out for fish and chips."

She raised her eyebrows and patted her belly.

"I know, I know. I'll get out on the bike as soon as this case is out of the way."

He heard the door open and Vivienne Bailey waved at him as she crossed the room and dragged a chair in front of his desk.

"I've got to go, Penny. I'll see you later."

"Don't mind me. I just thought I'd bring you some news," Bailey said.

"I appreciate it. You're working late?"

"Could say the same thing to you. Where are all your people?"

"I've sent them home. We're waiting for stuff from the Digital Forensics Lab. I'm hoping it'll give us a direction. Terry Denn's here somewhere."

"Oh, don't let that Denn bloke make me a coffee. Silly bugger, might put a love potion in it." She grinned at him and winked. "Anyway, I've sent you a video of the inside of the white van. It lit up nicely when we got the luminol and black light on it. Blood on the floor. We've sent samples off for type and DNA; it was dried so that should work."

Jordan opened the file and watched the white figure moving in the small interior of the van.

"It looks very clean."

"Yes, it'd been scrubbed out. Just like the kitchen at the victim's house. But, as you know, you just can't get rid of all the blood. It was in the crevices, round the edges and round the bolts and little scratches on the floor. He had used bleach to clean so that complicated matters but we were able to get enough to work with. There was nothing on the walls – no hand marks or smears – no way was the victim moving about in there. I would say it was transport of the body only. No spatter, no brain matter, just blood."

"No brain matter. What does that tell you? We know the injury to the head was extensive."

"It suggests to me that the body was already wrapped in some way. Blood will leak out, it gets everywhere. Makes our job easier, but brain matter not so much. Yes, if the head was laid directly on the floor and the van was jiggling and moving, it's possible loose bits of skull and brain could be shaken out but there was nothing like that. I reckon she was wrapped up and what we have are traces from the wrappings, possibly from the killer, who must have been covered in it, and anything he carried from the scene along with some seepage from the bag. Even though the wrapping was torn by its journey down the Mersey it wouldn't ever have been completely sealed. There would be leakage when it was moved."

"At least, I can tell DCI Cross with some certainty that we've found the killer of Beatrice Sharp. I guess we knew already, but it's good to have it confirmed. Thing is though, where does that leave me?"

"Floundering, Jordan, that's where I reckon it leaves you. Floundering. Do you fancy a drink?"

"No, I'd better not. I have to update my book and I want to go through reports from the Time Tracers' computers. Thanks though – soon, yeah. When we've got this squared away."

"I'm free." Terry Denn had come into the room to collect his coat at the end of the conversation.

"Ha, I thought you'd have better fish to fry, Detective Constable." She grinned at him as she spoke and he held up his hands, a gesture of surrender. "Come on then, get a move on. You can come and meet my friend Rebecca. You'll like her."

As they walked to the door Sergeant Bailey turned around.

"Oh yeah, a little bright spot for you, Jordan. There was a receipt for a burger and chips in Ben Harwood's wallet. I've sent a copy to the medical examiner – she should be able to give you a pretty good idea of time of death with the gloop from his stomach. Don't stay too late."

And with that she swept out and Jordan listened to her boots clomping down the corridor and the sharp burst of a laugh – it sounded like Terry. At least this latest news might mean he could avoid another trip to Bootle. There was nothing now that Ben's mother could tell them that would make much difference and she had a long and difficult road ahead. It would be a while before she could have her son's body, there would be an inquest and at the end of it all she had to come to terms with what he had done. The best that Jordan could do for her was to find out why.

Chapter 52

Penny was already in bed by the time Jordan admitted defeat and wound things up in the office. He had gone through copies of the printouts from Time Tracers over and over but there was so little of it that he could really understand that in the end he had to acknowledge he was wasting time. He had logged onto the company home page. Ben Harwood was still there as one of our 'Tracers' but it was only an image and his attempts to access any more information resulted in him being re-routed to Lipscowe himself.

He wasn't sure what he had hoped to find anyway. It was too specialised, and he had no access to deleted files and records. They had the laptop and phone and his call to the lab had sounded promising, but they stressed it would all take time.

* * *

When the call came next morning, he was enjoying a second cup of coffee with Penny and listening to her plans for the following week when she would be back in work. Harry was settling well in his nursery and he felt for a moment that life was moving on without him while he was mired in the search for the truth about Beatrice.

"Good morning, boss. DC Searle here. Sorry to bother you. We have had two calls this morning. The first was from the nursing home to tell us that Mrs Sharp died in the night. It was just a courtesy and I wouldn't have bothered you with that. But the second call was from one of the geeks down in the lab. He was very excited, says he has some really interesting information and wondered if you could call in there as soon as possible. Speak to George Phillips. He's expecting you."

"Excellent. I'm on the way."

Penny was watching him, her eyebrows raised in question, but it was too complicated to begin to explain so he simply pulled her to her feet and kissed her.

"I have a good feeling about this. I really do."

She crossed her fingers and held her hands up in front of her.

"Go on then. Go."

* * *

"You look exhausted, mate," Jordan said.

George glanced at his watch. "Yeah – I should probably go home. Get some zeds."

"Have you been here all night?"

"Yes. I was in the zone."

"Bloody hell, mate."

The technician grinned up at him.

"I'll crash later, probably sleep for twenty-four hours solid. Thing is though, when you're in the middle of stuff, it's gripping. I know how that sounds but I like my job so…" He shrugged.

"Well I for one am really grateful. What have you got for me?"

"Okay. Pull up a chair. Actually, this won't take long. He did have a go at hiding what he'd been up to but he wasn't clever enough for me. Anyway, long story short.

First of all, I contacted the owner of timetracers.com. He's nice, we had a good chat. He gave me remote access to parts of his system. To be honest we already knew what was on there and I didn't find anything extra hidden. So, then I went to your bloke's own laptop. He'd wiped the hard drive recently. It's not a problem, a large percentage of the machines we have are like that. We can retrieve more than people realise. Anyway, I found confirmation that he had interacted with someone who had the same name as your dead girl. Have we not got her computer?"

Jordan shook his head.

"Oh, shame. There were a few emails where Harwood agrees to do some research and get back to her. I accessed the stuff he had in the cloud, but it was just social interaction, some photographs – nothing of any real interest and nothing to do with the dead woman. She was looking for her father by the way – I suppose you knew that. Not bothered about any other family members, grannies or grandads. There was one response from her. Short, just an okay, thereafter he told her he would do it and quoted a price."

As Jordan leaned in to get a closer look, the technician lost himself in a huge yawn, reached out for a can of energy drink and took a long swallow. Jordan felt guilty, the bloke was obviously whacked but he needed this information, so he waited for him to continue.

"So, seems she didn't want anything beyond that one thing. Didn't want to know about her family background or anything. Not what you'd expect."

"That's interesting. Did they find him?"

"Ah, that's where it all became much more fun."

"How so?"

"The contact ended. The references disappear. There is just nothing." George leaned back and grinned.

Jordan couldn't keep the disappointment from his voice.

"So, that was it? I thought maybe there would be more."

Phillips rubbed his hands together and gave a small laugh.

"Ha, that was what I thought. I mean, what I found didn't seem enough to lead to all the blood and guts that you've been dealing with. Not boring you, am I?"

"No. Not yet." Jordan grinned at him.

"Okay, so I'll stop messing with you. I was sure there must be something else and I had noticed that there was a reference number against the emails. Nothing that made much sense at first glance, look."

Jordan read it out. "GTA.V 13. Doesn't mean anything to me, not straight away."

"Ah, no, I suppose it wouldn't to a clean-living lad like you. But to me it popped pretty quickly."

He picked up a plastic case and waved it in the air. By now Jordan was beginning to feel boggled. The room was filling with other technicians, there were machines booting up, early morning banter and the smell of coffee and bacon and now, this bloke was showing him a computer game. He took a breath and chewed on his lower lip. He shook his head.

Look – Grand Theft Auto V – ha, so obvious. With a flourish George took out the disc, made a tutting noise as he held it in his fingertips.

"Not much in the way of a code."

He inserted it into the machine and Jordan shuffled in his chair. He didn't like computer games, they bored him and really, this was not the time.

"Ta daa."

The screen was filled with text. Copies of emails, not even that many. There were a few tiny yellow folders and some JPEGs showed as mini thumbnails.

"I don't understand?" Jordan said.

"He thought he was a spy this bloke. Playing at Bond or something but really it was pretty infantile. He used a portable disc machine. The activity was remembered by Windows so I had an idea what to look for. Easy for him to get rid of the portable player, but it might be worth your while bearing in mind, it could indicate that he's got a portable hard drive also. Though there is no trail on his main machine indicating that. Anyway, he just hid this in his computer games collection. It has to be said that sometimes simple is best and you probably wouldn't have realised just with a visual search.

"Okay, so here we have several communications back and forth and I can tell you're itching to get away, so I'll cut to the chase. He thinks he's found her father. He's done a decent job. There are pictures here of newspaper articles from twenty years ago and – copies of police reports relating to a sexual assault. But he didn't let her know that. Not as far as I can tell. As I say maybe there's another drive somewhere. Seems peculiar to do all this and then not let her know what he's found. It's all dated a couple of weeks before her murder. Maybe he went to see her."

"Yes, we know he did. He bashed her over the head with a torch."

"Oh yeah, there is that." The technician nodded.

"Here, I've copied it all for you and now I'm going to sleep." Abruptly, George Phillips stood, handed Jordan a memory stick, tossed his empty can into the waste bin and walked out of the room.

Chapter 53

It took a while to gather together the information that he needed, and the incident room was full by the time Jordan arrived. He marched straight to the corner by the whiteboard, as a way of grabbing all the attention.

"Okay. We have some forward movement. We are now interested in one Graham Matthews. Information retrieved from Ben Harwood's computer, tells us that Matthews is very possibly Beatrice Sharp's father. He is probably in his late thirties now. Lived in the area twenty years ago. Now the nasty bit. He was accused of a sexual assault, rape actually, but all charges were dropped. The woman who accused him was Vera Sharp."

He waited for the muttering to die down.

"The historical report of the assault is brief, and I get the impression that the woman was not taken seriously. There are no medical reports and if they did interview this bloke it wasn't under caution. Just one reference to his name and no record of any follow-up. But there is mention of the incident in the newspaper, her name but not his. I know that's dodgy, we all know that, but it is what it is."

He saw the anger in the faces of women around the room.

"The officer involved retired about ten years ago and died last year. We have some images of Matthews on this stick. Beverly, could you do the honours."

He handed the memory stick to her and after some clicking and scrolling a decent picture of Graham Matthews appeared on the large screen.

"Now, as you see from the date stamp this is very recent. So, we have to assume that Ben Harwood definitely followed this man. Maybe he was in touch with him personally but as yet we haven't found any evidence of that. No emails or such like – and we haven't found anything on his mobile phone. However, we do have the image of Beatrice on the other phone, the one Harwood nicked from the bloke in the pub. Chances are he has used a succession of mobiles, either stolen or cheap burners, we don't know yet. But we will find out. DC Denn, you're with me. We are going to have a chat with Mr Matthews. DC Searle, could you carry on with the CCTV from the hotel. This is only one track and we still have to keep everything else alive."

"I've been through all of the hotel CCTV that was recorded on the day of Harwood's murder," Rosalind Searle said. "He went out early and came back with his meal in a bag. So, he was alive at eleven-thirty. The housekeeper noticed the blood on the carpet at just after five. It gives us a pretty tight timeline. The place is busy, people in and out all the time. Nobody obviously following him and nobody who seems to be loitering or behaving oddly. The CCTV in the public areas is fine but some of the cameras in the stairs and hallways could do with better siting. Anyway, his room door isn't clearly visible. There is some activity in the corridors and I'm going over it again now but generally during the day it's just people walking back and forth to the lifts, checking in and out. I intend to widen the search and see where else he went on his meal run. He was gone quite a long time just to pick up a takeaway. There are plenty of cameras in the area."

"At least now we have a good idea of who we might be looking for. As many of you as possible assist DC Searle. We need footage of Matthews down near the hotel."

"If he was there, I'll find him, boss."

Jordan turned back to the room.

"Listen, ladies and gents, I feel really strongly that this man, Graham Matthews, is relevant. He's a link between both victims and that's too important to ignore. If it helps, remember that he's probably a rapist who got away with it. Perhaps that anger will help to drive you. I need evidence of involvement. When I bring him in, I want to be able to take away any hope that he can squirm out of this. I reckon we may well have a killer out there who'll make a run for it if he can, someone who got away with violent crime once before – well not again, not if we can help it."

"Terry, I'm going down to see DCI Cross. I want an appeal out on the news. It's always busy down there by the Pier Head, there are plenty of tourists taking pictures. I am going to see if we can get some plods on the ground, bobbies with clipboards – it'll amuse the American Beatles fans at least."

They grabbed their coats and headed for the car park.

"You're stoked with this aren't you?"

"Yeah. It feels right," Jordan said.

"This bloke, you think he's killed Ben Harwood?"

"I have a gut feeling. They're definitely connected so we have to pick that up and run with it. It's all we have right now."

"But Ben Harwood was a killer too. We're about one hundred per cent certain he killed Beatrice."

"That's true. What's your point?"

Terry paused and looked down at his feet.

"It just seems that, maybe he, this Matthews bloke, did us all a favour."

"So, you think maybe we should just let him go?"

"No, not exactly…"

"What then?"

"Just seems to be a lot of effort?"

"I know where you're coming from. I do get it. Beatrice was, as far as we know, completely innocent. Ben Harwood was almost definitely a killer. But it's not our job to judge. It's our job to bring people to justice, yeah. That's it. If you start to make decisions about who can and can't break the law, you're treading a very dangerous path. Apart from anything else, we don't know what's happened yet, not for certain, but we have to find out, even if it's only to eliminate him from our enquiries."

"Sorry, boss. I've spoken out of turn."

"We have a job to do and really, it's quite simple. For me it is anyway. Bad guys can't win. Okay?"

Chapter 54

"Are you intending to bring him in?" Terry asked as they left the car and walked across the visitor's parking.

There was a chill wind blowing from the river, up between the pale stone buildings and Jordan pulled his jacket tighter around him.

"Let's just see, shall we? We need to be careful. No slip-ups that'll have the CPS turning up their noses."

The interior of the lovely old office building had been sympathetically upgraded and modernised and the spaces were brightly lit and impressive. A uniformed official behind the reception desk called ahead to let the investment company know they were about to have visitors. He knew better than to ask what the police were doing visiting in the middle of a workday, but as Jordan and Terry crossed the marble hallway he turned and raised his eyes at the girl sorting mail into pigeon-holes.

"Wonder what they've been up to on the fourth floor?"

"Probably haven't paid their parking fines," she muttered.

Upstairs the receptionist was insistent that Mr Matthews was in a meeting and couldn't be disturbed.

"It is essential that we speak to him and we can't hang around," Jordan said.

"I'm sorry, I don't know what you want me to do."

The young woman turned away with a flick of her sleek blond hair and went back to working on her computer. Terry leaned in close. It made Jordan smile as he noticed the thickening of the Scouse accent.

"Wha' we want, is for you to go and get your boss. Now. We need a word, awright, queen?"

She glared at the two men but pushed her chair away from the desk and clomped across the parquet floor.

Graham Matthews smiled as he walked towards them, his hand outstretched, but there was a tightness around his mouth and his palm was clammy.

"Gentlemen, what can I do for you?"

"Is there somewhere private we can talk?" Jordan said.

"Oh dear, that sounds ominous."

The attempt at a laugh came out sharp and brittle as he ushered them into an office, offered them coffee, which they refused, and sat down on a small sofa in front of the window. They took the chairs opposite. Jordan opened his folder and pulled out the morgue image they had of Ben Harwood.

"Do you know this man?"

Matthews made no attempt to take the printout, leaning forward and glancing briefly at the photograph.

He shook his head.

"No. Sorry, I don't. Is he dead? Only he looks as though he is."

"You've never met him?" Terry said, ignoring the question.

"Not that I remember. Am I supposed to have done? Is he a client?"

"Not as far as we know." Jordan pulled out a second piece of paper. "What about this woman, do you know her?"

Again, there was a brief shake of Graham Matthews' head as he pulled down the corners of his mouth. He glanced briefly at the picture of Beatrice and then up and out of the window.

"No, sorry. Never met her. Who are they?"

"I need to ask you where you were on Monday of this week, Mr Matthews, specifically Monday afternoon and evening?"

"Erm." Matthews swallowed audibly. "I was here. In work. In the evening I was at home with my wife."

"Were you here all day?"

"Yes. Started early and left late."

He tried for a laugh as he raised his hands palm upwards and shrugged his shoulders.

"You didn't go out at all?" Jordan asked.

"No, no – I don't think so. Oh, hang on, yes, I did. I went out at lunch time. Just for a breath of air. No point being down here on the waterfront without taking advantage. When the weather's decent anyway."

"Were you alone?"

"Yes. Just me."

"What time was that?"

"About twelve I think."

"And in the afternoon?"

"In the afternoon I had meetings. Two. They are in my diary. Look, just what is this about? Is there some sort of problem here?"

Again, they ignored his questions.

"Can anyone vouch for the fact that you were in meetings all afternoon on Monday, Mr Matthews?" Jordan said.

"Yes, as I say it's in my diary."

"But what about physical proof. What about someone who was with you?"

"Right. Of course. Both meetings were attended by several members of the board and they are minuted. Louise can show the minutes to you, but I'll need to get permission from someone senior first. But she was in there anyway. Just ask her – shall I call her in?"

"That would be helpful, thank you."

Jordan's mind was racing. They needed to get onto the morgue – see if they could be given an accurate time of death. He took out his phone and texted DC Searle back in the office.

"Are you sure you won't have a drink? This could take a couple of minutes."

Matthews opened the door and called the secretary. This was not going the way that Jordan had imagined.

Chapter 55

The atmosphere in the incident room was one of disbelief tinged with an edge of panic. They had all expected Jordan and Terry to bring Graham Matthews in for questioning under caution. They had been quietly confident that they were moving towards a conclusion. Everything appeared to be coming together. Two murders solved in quick succession, a stunning result and guaranteed big night at the pub.

Instead Jordan had asked them to get back on the computers.

"Okay, we have a narrow timeline," he said. "According to the medical examiner, and always assuming that he ate the food as soon as he arrived back in his room, Ben Harwood died in the early afternoon. Between two and six hours to digest it completely and the food was only partly digested. Of course, it's not absolute, there are many factors involved, but the medical examiner is pretty confident we are looking at between one and five which fits with when the housekeeper noticed the blood. Problem is that Graham Matthews was in meetings from two until after six o'clock. There is no question about that.

He was with another five colleagues and his name is mentioned in the minutes when he commented."

"What about breaks for the toilet. It's not that far from his office to the hotel?" Rosalind Searle said.

"It's a thought, but realistically, how long does it take to go for a pee," Terry answered.

"I need you to find him for me. I need proof that he was out of his office between twelve and two o'clock. There is more than one door to that building, there's plenty of CCTV coverage around there. We know he went out for a walk, he told us that, but we have confirmed that he came back again at just after twelve. I would like to see his first trip out just for the record, but that's not what I need now. Did he go out again? Did he meet someone? He says not. Come on guys, we need to find him or come up with something else entirely. I'm open to anything right now."

* * *

"Terry, I think we need to go back to the Wirral."

Jordan had been studying the notes in his book as Terry brought him a cup of coffee from the table in the corner. Nobody had yet managed to improve the drinks situation and the jar of powdered instant coffee was now clogged with lumps. They had given up on keeping fresh milk and all they had was coffee creamer, a generic brand from the mini supermarket nearby. Jordan took a sip.

"Jesus, that's bad. Okay. We're going out via the supermarket down the road. I'm getting us a coffee machine."

"I thought it was okay, to be honest. But, you know, I'm up for a change and I can give my mum her kettle back. Um, why are we going over to the Wirral again?"

"The strongest connection between all three principles in this case is timetracers.com. We have to be careful not to get too bogged down in what we think we know. I'll be honest, I thought we had this cut and dried but there is the real possibility that the timings don't work. So, we go back to the beginning. I want another chat with Mr Lipscowe. I know he seems like a really nice guy but so did Ted Bundy."

"Who?"

Jordan raised his eyebrows and stared at the detective constable.

"Okay, I'm going to pretend I didn't hear that. Look him up. Really, look him up." He picked up his jacket. "I'll meet you in the car park. We'll take my car, but I want to get a coffee from the machine in the hall. It's crap but it's better crap than this. Sorry."

* * *

At first, when he saw the cluster of people around his car, Jordan assumed they were friends of Terry's. Certainly, he was the centre of attention. As he approached, he realised that the interaction was far from friendly and Terry's voice was raised. He was pointing and shaking his head.

"Hey, what's going on?" Jordan put the cup of coffee on the top of a concrete bollard and marched across the tarmac.

Terry turned to him. "Boss, tell these idiots to back off."

The woman nearest to Jordan held up her warrant card.

"Internal Affairs. You are?"

"DI Jordan Carr. What's going on?"

"Is this officer on your team, sir?"

"Yes, we're on our way out. We're in the middle of a serious investigation. I'll ask you again, what is going on?"

"You're going to have to manage without DC Denn, I'm afraid. We need him to come with us."

"Boss." Terry's voice was tight with anger.

"Sorry, DI Carr. There's been a complaint against this officer, we have to ask you to release him from whatever you were doing right now. You'll have to use someone else," the woman said.

"Why, what is he supposed to have done?" As he asked the question Jordan knew there would be no answer.

She simply shook her head. "Sorry."

There were three of them and although they didn't use handcuffs, they made it impossible for Terry to go anywhere except the way that they herded him. Back towards the building.

Jordan was left literally scratching his head and as they passed through the narrow gap at the entrance, the coffee cup was knocked, spinning to the floor where it lay in a forlorn pool of cooling brown liquid.

"Absolutely, bloody brilliant," Jordan said as he picked it up and flung it towards the waste bin.

Chapter 56

As he stormed back to the incident room, Jordan phoned ahead.

"DC Searle, I want you to come with me. I'm going to have a word with Stan Lipscowe."

"Oh right, I thought DC Denn was with you, sir."

"Change of plan."

He opened the door to find a cluster of people gathered around Rosalind's desk.

"Hello, what's happening?"

"We think we've got a sighting of him – Graham Matthews. It's the first trip out but it looks like he did meet with someone after all."

Rosalind pointed at her screen as the others moved aside to let Jordan in.

"There. The bloke in the black hoody. The one by the statue of John. I thought he was behaving oddly, first of all he kept putting his briefcase down, picking it up, several times, looks edgy. Plus, he's wearing suit trousers and leather shoes with a scruffy hoody. I know that doesn't really mean much but it drew my attention. Anyway, if we move on…" She moved further along the timeline. "Now, there we have this other bloke – looks like Matthews. They don't appear to have a conversation. It looks like a quick greeting and then they move away. Of course, sod's law they then go out of shot and we don't know what happened. But then Graham Matthews comes back across the concourse and we pick him up again at the offices. I'm almost certain it's him. I know it doesn't tell us much, but we do know now that he lied."

"We do. Well done, Rosalind. I don't suppose there is a clearer view of the person he met?"

"Haven't found one yet but we are on it now. Is DC Denn okay?"

"Yup." Jordan turned away before she could ask him any more questions. "In view of this I think I'll hold off the trip over the water. I'm going to have another word with Mr Matthews. You're with me. Thank you, everyone. Please keep on with this. I still need Matthews out of his office a second time."

* * *

The same secretary gave them the same snotty look as Jordan and Rosalind Searle stepped up to her desk.

"Yes, can I help you?"

They had automatically taken out their warrant cards, but she didn't bother to look up from her screen.

"Graham Matthews," Jordan said.

There was a silent stand-off as the girl continued to type; eventually she turned her head. She sighed.

"Gone home."

"It's a bit early, isn't it?" Jordan asked. He glanced at his watch.

"Not my business." The secretary turned back to her keyboard.

* * *

"My nan lives in Garston," Rosalind Searle told Jordan as they drove out to the suburb. "It's nice. Just houses really, but lots of trees and not far from the promenade. I used to love coming here when I was a kid."

"We haven't had the chance to have much of a chat, Rosalind. I'm sorry about that," Jordan said. "We will make time when things calm down a bit. But I do want you to know that I'm impressed with the work that you've been doing."

"Thanks, boss. I appreciate that." She looked down at her lap, a little embarrassed. "Can I ask? What's going on with Terry?"

"I think it's best if we don't discuss that just yet. Unclear exactly what's happening, he was needed somewhere else. Anyway, here we are. Let's go and have a word with Mr Matthews. See what he says about telling us porkies."

Chapter 57

The blinds shifted on the front window. Jordan rang the bell again and thumped with the side of his fist on the door.

"What the hell?" Matthews glared at them. He was still wearing his office clothes but he was in his socks and had loosened his tie. "Oh, it's you again. What the blazes do you want now? This is not on. I shall make a complaint."

"If we could come in for a minute, Mr Matthews. This might not take very long."

"No, I don't want you in my home. Tell me what you want and then go away."

"In that case, Mr Matthews, we are going to have to ask you to come with us to the station. Do you want to put your shoes on?"

It did the trick, the man's face drained of all colour and he stepped back into the hallway.

"Oh, for God's sake. Come in. What the hell is it you want? I told you I didn't know that bloke. What more can I say?"

Though they were now inside he made no attempt to move along the hallway and he left the front door open. Jordan held up the printout taken from the video.

"Is that you, sir?"

Matthews snatched the picture from his hand and glanced at it.

"No, that's not me."

"Could you look at it again? I believe it is you, and that, contrary to what you told us, you did meet with someone on Monday, at the Pier Head. Now, if you can explain who that was and what the meeting was about, we can let you get on with your evening."

Graham Matthews held out his hand, he took the image and, after glancing at the picture again he handed it back. His hand was shaking and sweat moistened his forehead.

"No, I told you, it's not me. I was in work all day."

"You told us you went out for a walk."

"Okay yes, but just a walk. Not a meeting. Look, just go away and leave me alone, otherwise I'm going to get my lawyer down here and we'll be submitting a formal complaint."

They heard a car slow in the road, then the clunk as it crossed the kerb to turn into the drive.

"That's my wife. She's just coming home from work. I don't want her upset. She's expecting."

They turned to watch the woman climb out of the car; she wasn't obviously pregnant and moved easily as she leaned into the rear seat to take out a sports bag. She smiled at them as she crossed the narrow driveway and stopped on the front step.

"Hello. Sorry we are really not interested in religion."

"They're not Witnesses, love. It's the police."

"Oh, her hand flew to her mouth. What's happened, is it my mum?"

"Don't upset yourself, Mrs Matthews." As she spoke Rosalind Searle moved nearer to the woman. "We are just here to talk to your husband."

"Oh, thank God." She laughed now. "Look, come on in. Why are you hanging around in the doorway?" She turned sideways to squeeze past them, kissed her husband on the cheek. "Come in, please."

They trooped into the house. Rose Matthews flung her bag on the floor and kicked off her shoes.

"Right, does anyone want a drink – tea, coffee, something cold?"

The atmosphere had changed too suddenly, Graham Matthews looked panicked and unbalanced.

"They're not staying, love. They just wanted to ask me something and I've already answered them. They're going now."

"Oh."

Jordan held out the picture. "We were trying to ascertain whether or not this is your husband."

Rose glanced at it, then at her husband. She didn't speak.

"Mrs Matthews?" Jordan said.

"Sorry, sorry. I need the loo. I'm pregnant, it's a bugger, when you've got to go, you know you just have to go. Nice to meet you." She turned and took the short walk along the hall to a narrow door under the stairs.

"Now, you really need to leave us alone," Matthews said.

If they took him in now it could backfire, this wasn't enough. They all knew that it was him in the photograph but Ben Harwood had been seen after the meeting going back to the hotel, all too alive, and Matthews had gone back to his office. They had unnerved him, there had been no doubt, but it just wasn't enough.

"I think we will need to speak to you again, Mr Matthews. In the meantime, if you want to get in touch, here's my card. I suggest you give this some thought. If you want to come in and see us at any time, to clear this up, then just get in touch and I'll make sure I'm available."

They pulled away from the kerb.

"Do you think we'll get a search warrant, boss?" Rosalind said.

214

"Not with what we have. The biggest problem is that Harwood was definitely still alive after he met with Matthews on the Pier Head. If we can't prove he left his office for a second time, it's going nowhere. Shit."

Chapter 58

"Are you alright?" Rose Matthews knelt before her husband. He sat on the settee his head buried in his hands; when he looked up there were tears on his face.

"No, I'm not alright. I'm not alright. I'm a wreck. They came into work. The boss wanted to know why police were wanting to talk to me. He wanted to know if it was to do with the company. Of course it isn't, bloody idiot. They wouldn't have talked to me if it was. They would have gone straight to the top. Anyway, he's now having someone audit all my accounts. For the whole bloody time I've worked there. All those years and one little visit from the police and he wants to audit my accounts."

"But you've got nothing to worry about there, have you?"

As he answered her, he felt bile rise in his throat.

"No, of course not."

It had been so close. He should be counting his blessings that he'd dodged the bullet, that he'd made sure everything was the way it should be. Christ, he hoped he hadn't missed anything. It was too late now if he had. His accounts were closed to him until after the audit.

"He told me to take tomorrow off. I told him it was a mistake, but he's so tight-arsed."

"It'll be alright, love."

"I know, but what about this other thing. He's dead. Did you know he's dead? Christ you didn't, did you?"

"Who is?"

"That bloke, that blackmailer. That's why they came into the office. Somebody killed him."

"Oh Lord. That's awful, isn't it?"

"It's more than awful. They're looking at me for it. Oh, they keep saying they're not, that they only want to talk to me. But they have that picture. You could tell they thought it was me. They're going to have me for murder."

He gave a laugh. It was verging on hysteria. Rose sat beside him and wrapped her arms around his shoulders.

"Don't panic. You didn't kill him, did you?"

He turned to stare at her. "No, I didn't kill him. How can you even say that? How can you even think that?"

"I didn't, I wasn't, it was – oh what's the word… rhetorical. Anyway, as I say, you didn't kill him so just keep calm and it'll all be okay."

"No, no it won't. They'll find out about that girl and that'll just make it worse. See, I should have known this would happen. I tried to fix things, tried to make it go away and it's become worse and worse and now it's all going to come out anyway. I'll have to go away."

"What the hell do you mean?"

"I'll have to go, leave the country. They're going to accuse me of murder. At the least it'll come out about what I did, to that bloody woman. That'll make me look bad and that'll be it, they'll have me for murder. Jesus, what am I going to do?"

"And what about me?"

"What?"

"Me, me and the baby. What about us? If you run away, what happens to us?"

"I suppose I'll have to get things sorted out and then you can follow. Spain probably. I can go to Spain. Yes, yes. There are loads of English people there, rich ones and I can set up in business and you can come and join me. It'll be good. We can leave all this mess behind."

"Don't talk so bloody daft. I'm not going to Spain. Just calm down, Graham. Don't be such a wimp. All you have to do is stick to the story. Just keep telling them that it wasn't you. They mustn't have enough evidence to prove you had anything to do with it, otherwise they'd have arrested you. Just calm down and pour us both a drink."

"You're not supposed to drink."

"Pour me a bloody drink. I need to think."

Chapter 59

Terry Denn was in the incident room when Jordan and Rosalind arrived. The civilians were packing up and leaving and until they had all gone, he didn't speak. He was fiddling with his phone and didn't look at anyone until the room was empty.

He glanced at Rosalind Searle and she took the hint.

"Right, boss. I'm off, back in tomorrow early. See you, Terry."

"So, what's going on?" Jordan asked as the door closed behind her.

"Sorry, boss. I've been suspended pending investigation. I'm not supposed to be here right now to be honest, but I wanted to see you myself. I suppose they'll speak to you tomorrow."

Jordan pulled a chair towards the desk and sat opposite his detective constable. He rubbed the back of his neck and flexed his shoulders.

"What's it about, this investigation?"

"Complaint from some woman geggin' in. Says they saw me giving some lad a seeing to."

As Terry became more distressed, he became more and more Scouse, Jordan had trouble understanding.

"Hang on. Do you want to tell me in plain English?"

"Yeah, sorry, boss. Some nosey woman up near my mam's said she saw me beating up her nephew. So, she put in a complaint. Police brutality, she said."

"And did you?"

There was a moment of silence.

"No, I didn't but I'm glad he got what was coming to him. You can't go round mugging old women. This gobshite hit my mam, pinched her stuff and left her with her face all bruised."

"You know the correct way to deal with that is to report it. I told you at the time, didn't I?"

"Yeah. But there was no point. This is so bloody unfair, just because we're from Kirkby. You don't know what it's like."

"I don't know what it's like? What, you mean living somewhere tough, somewhere you have to watch your back all the time, somewhere you might get into trouble through no fault of your own simply for being who you are, for what you look like? Oh no, I wouldn't know anything about that, would I? Christ, Terry, have you ever looked at me? Of course I know. You stupid sod. You do realise that this could ruin any chance of a decent career. You could be thrown out for this. You probably will be. I suppose the evidence against you is pretty solid?"

"She knows about what happened to my mam. She knows me. But honestly, I didn't do it. I reckon it's all just sour grapes. I told them I didn't do it."

"What did the union representative suggest?"

"He was about as much use as a chocolate teapot to be honest. Just said to think about how I'm going to explain myself. Try to minimise the damage if I can."

"Are you going to get a solicitor?"

"No. Yes. Oh, I don't know. Thing is I reckon this could have been– well, let's say somebody I know. It wasn't me. I can tell you think it was, but it wasn't."

"You had bruises, scratches on your hands."

"Yeah."

"What were they from?"

"Skateboarding."

"What?"

"Skateboarding. Okay, I know. Bloody juvenile. Thing is though, I love it, always have done and I go down the skate park sometimes. I lark about with the kids down there. It's relaxation and it shows that we're not all just what they call pigs, the filth, bizzies – we have a laugh. I knew you'd have taken the piss if I'd told you. You and all the others. But it's relaxing and I reckon it's doing some good."

"And you really didn't do this?"

"No, boss. I didn't."

"Okay, we'll just have to convince them."

"Yeah, that could be complicated. Might not be as straightforward as it seems."

"Only you can decide, but do what you can, Terry. I could do with you back here. This case is not working out the way I'd hoped and we're really short of bums on seats. If there's a way that you can make this go away – at least consider it, yeah. I'll do what I can tomorrow. I'll have a word with DCI Cross."

"Right, thanks, boss."

Chapter 60

DCI Cross was less than sympathetic. Jordan had phoned on the way in to make an appointment and been promised ten minutes.

"I can't interfere, this is an internal affairs matter now and you know how that works. It's out of my hands."

"Is there no way we can bring him back in, though?"

"Don't be ridiculous, you know that's not going to happen. Look, leave that alone and get back to your murder. I'm under pressure all ways round here and don't have anything much to tell the top brass. Your last report was pretty thin. How far have you got with this bloke in Garston?"

"We interviewed him yesterday. He's still in the frame. It's a timing problem more than anything. I've got everyone on it."

"Best concentrate on that and leave DC Denn to the rubber heelers. Now, if there's nothing else…"

* * *

Terry Denn rang, as Jordan had known he would.

"Any luck, boss? What did DCI Cross say?"

"Sorry, Terry, there's nothing he can do. In fairness I guess we knew that. Honestly, the only thing now is wait. Unless you can find a way to prove you didn't do it."

"Give me something to do, boss. I can't just hang around at home. My mam's giving me down the banks for getting into trouble, it's doing my head in."

"You know I'm not supposed to do that."

"Please."

"Look, leave it with me. If there's anything that comes up that we might get away with, I'll let you know."

"Cheers, boss."

Beverly Powell was waiting in the office with a sheet of paper in her hand.

"Report from the medical examiner on Ben Harwood, sir."

"Did you need to print it? I could have read it online."

As he heard himself Jordan was swept with irritation. This stuff was all so bloody unimportant when he had two dead bodies and no real progress. What was he turning into?

"Sorry, Beverly. Thanks for this. I've been having a sod of a morning."

"Can I make you a drink?"

"God, no." They both laughed.

"Probably best," she said. "That report is a preliminary but when they sent it through, Dr Grant said she'd be happy to talk to you if you had any questions."

Though they were still waiting for the toxicology results, the report was thorough. Much of it was what they already knew. A knife with no serrations, probably twenty centimetres narrowing to a point. In other words, she had added, a knife from just about any kitchen these days. The angle of penetration suggests a right-handed assailant about the same height as the victim.

Jordan pulled up the original report which had Harwood at one point seven five meters. Not particularly tall for a man. It was another blow, though. Graham

Matthews was as tall as Jordan himself. One point nine. The difference was too big. The truth was becoming unavoidable. Graham Matthews was not the killer. He gave himself a moment for his mind to settle. It was a blow, no getting around it, but there was no time to beat himself up over it. They had to move on.

"DC Searle, you're with me. We're going over to Time Tracers. Meet me in the car park in ten."

Chapter 61

"Is everything okay with Terry, boss?" Rosalind asked.

"No, not really but I don't think we can help him. I can't talk about it either."

They were almost at the tunnel entrance when Jordan's phone rang. It was on hands free and he stabbed at the button on his steering wheel.

"Boss, Terry here. Listen I'm outside the Matthewses' house."

"Why?"

"Aw come on – I told you, I was going mental at home. I just thought I'd come up here, see if there was anything to see. You'll be glad I did."

"Why?" Jordan said again.

"He's leaving. Packing up. Suitcases in the car."

"Shit."

"I know. What do you want me to do?"

"You can't do anything."

Jordan swung around the traffic island and headed down Dale Street, along Strand Street and towards the A562.

"Don't approach him, Terry, don't you dare. You're suspended. I'm on the way."

"You'd better get a shift on, boss. He's packed the car. He's back in the house now but I reckon he's ready to go."

Traffic was heavy as they raced through the centre and down towards the river. Jordan couldn't in all conscience use the integral blue lights, he leaned on the horn a couple of times. If he got a ticket, he reckoned he'd be able to talk his way out of it, but they didn't now have a valid reason to suggest that Graham Matthews was a person of interest. Everything they had heard in the last couple of days told them that he had nothing to do with Ben Harwood's murder. And yet, there was something, there had to be. He was involved and now he was leaving.

"Find out what's happening," he said to DC Searle. "Terry's on speed dial."

Terry answered the call immediately.

"Boss, he's on his way. I'm following."

"Which way is he heading? We're on the A561 – give me some directions," Jordan said.

"We're heading towards Widnes, probably the motorway. Head for the M62. I'll stay behind him."

"If he reaches the motorway, we're in trouble. I can't initiate a full-on pursuit. We haven't got enough on him to initiate one. Damn. Where are you?"

"We're heading down Speke Boulevard. It's busy, he's caught in the traffic."

"Yeah, so are we."

"Turn left here, boss," Rosalind yelled. Jordan glanced across the car. She was staring out of the windscreen but had her phone in her hand with the Google map open. "Left at the junction onto the A562 – left, left."

She seemed to know what she was doing so Jordan gave it over to her. They sped down Higher Road.

"Are you in your own car, Terry?" Jordan yelled.

"Yes, the blue Astra Sport. Matthews is in a silver Jag. We've just passed the Knowsley Expressway. Traffic is still heavy. He's not speeding, it's too congested. I reckon he's heading for the bridge. But he has no idea I'm following him."

"Have you got his plate number."

"Yep. I'm just a couple of cars behind him."

"Okay, give the registration to Rosalind. DC Searle, contact traffic. Report him for running a red light. Have them watch for him and tell them we're on the way. There'll be hell to pay after this, but I want to know why he's making a run for it and we need to stop him before he hits the motorway."

Chapter 62

Graham was stopped by a traffic patrol on the approach to the Mersey Gateway Bridge at Widnes. Jordan had been patched through to the officers on the ground.

"I'll be with you in a few minutes. Can you hold him there?"

"We can, but where was the offence committed? Have you got it on dash cam?"

He couldn't lie to them, that would be wrong. Though actually he had already done that, hadn't he?

"It's complicated. Just keep him there."

"Okay. Ah, is this you in the blue Vauxhall?"

"No. No, that's a colleague but he won't be involved."

"Right."

The traffic officer sounded hesitant and confused. They could hear his partner in conversation, voices were raised, and they assumed Graham Matthews was complaining about being stopped. He knew he hadn't committed a traffic offense and was very likely puzzled and annoyed.

"There, boss."

Rosalind Searle pointed to the small group pulled into a bus stop on the approach to the bridge. Jordan drew in behind them. Though he was there, Terry had stayed in his car; he was filming the confrontation on his mobile and Jordan frowned at him and shook his head. He didn't want any proof that a suspended detective had been involved in this situation which was going to take some explaining already.

He walked towards the traffic officers, his warrant card held in front of him.

"Thanks, guys. I'll take it from here."

Rosalind had taken the second officer to one side and was deep in conversation, Jordan hoped she'd be able to smooth things over. Graham Matthews took one glance at Jordan and then rested his arms on top of the car his head lowered into his hands.

Whatever DC Searle said did the trick and with a quick wave and a whispered conversation, the traffic officers clambered back into their car, pulled onto the carriageway, and drove off.

Jordan nodded at the DC and she gave him a quick smile.

"Mr Matthews. Are you going somewhere?"

"What's going on here? What's it got to do with you?"

"We have a few more questions for you and we really would prefer that you hang around for a while."

"You have no power to keep me here. You've got no good reason to pester me like this."

He was right and Jordan had to be careful. He couldn't take him in for questioning under caution, he certainly couldn't arrest him, but he couldn't let him go.

"We would very much like you to help us with our enquiries, Mr Matthews. We know that you had contact with Ben Harwood, we know that you met him very shortly before he was unlawfully killed. You can see how we might be interested in anything that you have to tell us."

He was bluffing. He just had to hope that Matthews wasn't too clued up on his rights.

"I've nothing to tell you. You've caused me trouble at work. Because of you, my boss is looking at my accounts. I've never done anything wrong in my business dealings, never, and yet now I'm being audited. It's your fault, all yours. You had no right to come into my place of business."

"Maybe we can help with that," Jordan said.

"What? How?"

"Maybe we could have a word with your boss. Tell him that we are not interested in your business dealings. Explain that it was another matter entirely. Would that be helpful?"

Matthews paced back and forth beside the car.

"So, shall we go now and have a word? It won't take long."

"No. I don't think it'll help. I don't want you talking to my boss, ever. Anyway, I've got nothing to hide, let them do their audit. I don't care."

While they were speaking, DC Searle peered into the Jaguar.

"You seem to have been planning a long holiday, Mr Matthews. Is that wise? You know, while there are problems at work. I would have thought you'd need to keep yourself in touch, be available. Might look a bit odd, you leaving right now."

"I've been under a lot of stress. I need to get away."

"I really would prefer you to stay in Liverpool, Mr Matthews. Until all this has been sorted out."

Jordan had no power to insist and if Matthews called his bluff, he would have to let him go. Matthews' phone rang. He dragged it out of his pocket, glanced at the screen and answered.

"Oh shit. Where are you now? I'm coming. I'm on my way."

"Everything okay?" Jordan asked.

"No, it's bloody not. My wife has been taken to the Women's Hospital. There's a problem with the baby. I have to go."

He didn't wait for them to speak. He clambered into his car and left them in a cloud of grit and dust as he headed across the bridge.

"That's lucky," Jordan said. "Stopped him in his tracks."

"Not lucky for his wife. Poor woman. I hope she'll be okay," Rosalind said.

As Graham Matthews drove away, Terry joined them at the side of the road.

"So, what's happening?"

"His wife's not well. He's been called to the hospital," Jordan told him

"Oh, that's lucky," Terry said.

"Bloody hell, what are you like?" Rosalind was angry.

"All I meant was…"

"It's okay, Terry, we know what you meant," Jordan said.

DC Searle took a step away, distancing herself from her male colleagues.

"Look, the main thing is to keep an eye on Matthews. I need to come up with a good reason to haul him in to have a word. I reckon he's pretty screwed up and if we keep on at him, he's going to make a mistake and incriminate himself. We know he didn't kill Harwood but he knows things that we need to get at. I can't shake the feeling that he's the key to all of this. Terry, will you take Rosalind to the Women's Hospital? Don't go in yourself, you have to stay at arm's length. If you're seen to have been involved here the whole thing could come down around our ears.

"I'm going back to the office. I'm going through everything again. I need to find what we're missing. I know they probably won't tell you anything at the hospital but hang around. See if you can find Matthews. Assess what the situation is. A sick wife, a baby in trouble. We really need to tread carefully. Especially as all we have is a gut feeling that he's at the bottom of all this – in all honesty, just my gut feeling."

"I'll do what I can, boss." Rosalind Searle turned and followed Terry back to his car.

Chapter 63

It was coming apart at the seams. The civilian assistants were marking time. Terry was suspended. Jordan's main suspect had become unsafe. He was losing it. It could only be a matter of time before DCI Cross called him in and took him off the case.

Once he was back in the office and thinking more calmly, Jordan re-assessed the situation. Why was Matthews running? He had a pregnant wife. Why would he leave her? Could it be because of the audit? Not if what he said was true and he had nothing to fear. It came back again to Ben Harwood, timetracers.com and Beatrice. It had to.

Well he couldn't run now, not if the pregnancy was at risk. Yes, it had been a thoughtless comment back there at the side of the road, but the situation did work in their favour. He'd have to support her. She'd need looking after. Maybe Rose Matthews would have to give up her job until after the baby came. For sure a personal trainer would need to be fit. Strong. More so than the average woman. He felt a tingle in the back of his neck as the small hairs raised.

He went through the CCTV footage of the meeting on the Pier Head again, right from the beginning. His phone rang and he let it go to voicemail.

He slowed the video, flipped back and forth. He watched Graham Matthews and the little pantomime with his briefcase. The approach by the figure that just had to be Ben Harwood, and then Matthews crossing the concourse back to his office. Just a little later Ben with his lunch bag heading back to the hotel. He altered the view so that the screen showed more of the area. It was busy. There were tourist groups, shoppers, businesspeople. He leaned in, played the footage a couple more times. Their focus had been too narrow, now it was obvious. Not a needle in a haystack at all and not a bloke in a scruffy hoody and business shoes. Not that at all.

* * *

Rosalind Searle left her message. The boss had probably gone home. There was no need to bother him. He looked worn out.

"It's okay, boss. She's been discharged. I did try to get some information, pretended it was my sister, all that rot, but they weren't having it. Just told me to speak to her directly. I hung around the car park as they left, close as I dared. It didn't look to me as though she knew he was planning on leaving. There was a lot of waving and pointing and 'there, there' gestures. I'm in a taxi now. I'm following, going to see if they go straight home."

The Matthews didn't look like a couple relieved to have been discharged from the hospital. Rosalind was close behind them as they turned into the driveway. The taxi driver had laughed when she asked him to follow the silver car. She'd made up a story about wanting to give them time alone after a drama.

"Not my business, love," he'd said. "Gives me something to tell the lads back in the office though."

When they arrived home, Rose flung herself out of the car and stormed up the path. She entered the hall and left the door swinging on its hinges behind her. Graham Matthews slumped after her. He had pulled one of his suitcases out of the boot and lugged it with him.

Once she'd paid for the taxi and given him time to drive away, Rosalind turned and walked back on the other side of the road. She stood beside an old oak tree growing in the grass verge. From there she could see the Matthewses' house.

The lights came on in two of the rooms downstairs. Graham came back out to the car, removed the second of his suitcases, pulling it behind him along the path and bouncing it up the steps.

Rosalind crossed the road and stood behind a fence and a privet hedge. She could see into the kitchen and part of the living room, providing they didn't close the curtains.

Rose was at the worktop pouring a glass of juice. She began to drink and turned as Graham came through the door. He spoke but it was impossible for Rosalind to hear what he was saying from so far away. He raised his hand in a defensive movement and patted at the air. Rose turned and flung the tumbler of juice across the room. The crash was audible from outside as the glass shattered against the wall. Graham stepped forward, his arms open in front of him.

Rose stretched across the countertop to a knife block. She pulled out the large chef's knife and turned back to her husband, brandishing the blade in front of her.

Rosalind ducked beneath the hedge and scuttled into the Matthewses' garden. She crouched under the kitchen window where she could hear the raised voices and by bobbing her head up could watch the scene going on inside.

She pulled out her phone and her fingers flew across the buttons.

Trouble at the Matthewses'. Knife involved. Need advice.

She clicked send and moved along the path to the rear door. She could go in and try to diffuse the situation, or she could wait until the boss responded to her text.

She didn't know what to do. She was a little afraid. An angry woman and a knife were not a good mix. On the other hand, surely, Rose Matthews had no gripe with her. Whatever the problem, it was between the woman and her husband. But she had reason to believe there was a life in danger. Her training told her that she should intervene. She had the right to enter the premises. Her training also told her that she shouldn't act on her own, shouldn't risk her life if there was any other way. But there was a pregnant woman in a terrible state inside and a man in danger. She had to do something.

Did she have the guts?

Chapter 64

Jordan heard the phone chime in his pocket. He was staring at the computer screen, watching the hotel reception area, waiting for the figure of Rose Matthews as she left. Just one more woman in the bustle of tourists. There was a bag slung across her body. She was wearing the jacket that had been tied around her waist by the sleeves as she strode across in front of the Liver Building. It was now zipped tightly, and she had pulled a peaked cap over her hair. It could be simply to alter her appearance but if they could find that jacket and the T-shirt she had on underneath, it would be covered in Ben Harwood's blood. He was sure of it.

He pulled out his phone, he needed to know just where she was now. If she was still in hospital, he would need to be circumspect about how he handled her. No matter where she was, it was time to speak to her. There was a missed call from DC Searle and a text. He opened the text.

He tried to call her back, listened to the voicemail. He typed on the tiny keyboard as quickly as he could. *Don't go in. Wait for backup.* There was no response.

He grabbed his jacket and ran from the building, screaming out of the car park with his integral blue lights flashing and his horn blaring.

He could call for backup, mobilise cars in the area, fill the road with the scream of sirens. Was there enough in her text to warrant that – what the hell did '*knife involved*' mean?

Jordan glanced at the dashboard clock. It was after seven, the rush hour should be over. He could risk driving through the outskirts of the city, it would be quicker. He'd plugged the phone into the hands-free device and he called her number. There was no answer. He left a voicemail, there was no real point, he knew that, but wanted to reach out, to let her know that help was coming.

* * *

Graham Matthews had moved across the kitchen towards his wife. He was speaking to her but so quietly Rosalind couldn't hear him. He still had his arms spread open in front of him. Maybe this was just a domestic argument and she should stay out of it. Interfering could ratchet up the situation – make Rose act either against him or against them both. The woman was wagging the knife back and forth, crying now, her face red, her hands shaking. Graham moved nearer. There wasn't much distance between them. He was reaching for the knife, still speaking.

The change was sudden and shocking. Rose Matthews went from a weeping wreck to a screaming harridan in the blink of an eye. Now Rosalind could hear her. The words were indistinct, but the distress, the anger was clear. She ran to the back door, hammered with the side of her fist.

"Police. Open the door." There was a brief silence. Rosalind rattled the doorknob. "Let me in."

She hammered again. Leaned and tried to make out what was happening through the patterned glass. There was a small window beside the door; Rosalind tried to see into the kitchen. Rose, half turned, glared towards the source of the noise. Graham Matthews looked up and saw Rosalind peering through the narrow pane. He shook his head.

Rose swivelled back to her husband. She took two steps across the kitchen floor jabbing at him with the blade. He dodged and ducked, he turned and tried to run for the hall door. Rosalind was hammering with the end of her ASP against the glass. Inside she heard Graham Matthews scream.

She struck the window with the end of the baton, but the double glazing was toughened. She drew back her arm and hammered again, all the strength of her upper body behind it. The window exploded in a shower of tiny pieces. Rosalind heard Graham scream again.

Chapter 65

As the glass shattered, Rose Matthews turned to see DC Searle reach her hand through the broken window. She yanked on the handle releasing the lock and flung the door back against the wall.

"Okay, Mrs Matthews, Rose, just put the knife down. Come on, love, this isn't helping anything."

"Get out – out – out."

The woman screeched and ran across the kitchen towards Rosalind. There was no sign of Graham. Rose was jabbing with the weapon in front of her. Rosalind stepped backwards pulling the door behind her, slamming it just as the screaming woman stabbed with the knife. There was a dull thud as the blade stuck in the wood.

"Christ." Rosalind had run backwards across the narrow patio, her baton raised, her heart pounding. She stopped. "Shit, shit." Her hands were shaking, she couldn't breathe. There was a moment of silence and then the door was dragged open and Rose Matthews appeared in the doorway. She had grabbed another knife and crouched forwards glaring out into the garden.

"Go away. Leave us alone. This is none of your business."

"Mrs Matthews, come on. You don't need to do this. Think of the baby, you should be taking things easy. This isn't going to do either of you any good. Calm down."

Rosalind lowered her arm, held the ASP at her side. This woman was taller, probably stronger than she was, she was angry and out of her mind. The odds in a fight were on her side and the best thing was to try and calm her down. Maybe the boss had read her message, maybe one of the neighbours had heard the smash of the window. Maybe help was on the way. But she didn't know.

Rose Matthews had left the house and was stalking across the garden to where Rosalind stood.

"Come on now, Mrs Matthews. We can sort this out. Let's talk about it. Let's go back in the house and have a chat."

It was impossible to tell if the words were getting through. Rosalind was stepping backwards towards the grass. She didn't dare turn away.

The figure of Graham Matthews appeared in the kitchen. He was staggering across the tiles, his hands clutched in front of his chest. He paused beside the table and leaned on the wooden top. Blood smeared across the surface as he lowered to a chair and doubled forward. They could hear him groaning. Rose turned and glanced back into the house.

"You stupid sod. Now, look what you've done. This is all your fault," she screeched.

She turned back to Rosalind who was motionless at the edge of the grass. She had seen a shadow in the side passage. She could hear the wail of sirens in the distance. The boss was here. It was all going to be okay. All she had to do now was keep this woman talking – just a little while longer.

Rose crossed the flags, the knife waving in front of her. She was sobbing, tears and snot running across her face. She raised a hand and wiped the mess away.

"He's a coward. A coward and a rapist. What about that? My husband is a rapist and a weak dirty little quitter. We're having a baby – how can I let him bring up my baby? It wasn't enough that he let us down. He was running away like the snivelling coward that he is. I'll tell you what though, it's not happening. He needed to stay and look after us, he's got responsibilities. We were going to be a proper family. I told him to fix it. He didn't, so I had to. Same as always, eh. We've got to sort things, don't we?" She wagged a hand back and forth between herself and Rosalind. "Women, always having to fix things."

Jordan stepped around the corner into the garden.

"How did you fix it, Rose? What did you do?"

She turned to face him, but her head twisted back and forth trying to watch all of them.

"Why don't we go in the house, Rose? You can tell us what you did, and we can help you to put things right."

As he spoke Jordan stepped closer. Rosalind watched him, waiting for the moment to help him. The knife was pointed straight at him now, just a metre away. She didn't know what he wanted her to do.

"How did you fix it, Rose? I know you went to the hotel. I've seen you on the video."

"Ha. Yes, I had to go. I knew he'd screw it up." She waved towards the kitchen. "I followed him. I saw him hand my money over to that idiot boy. What a loser. Greedy and stupid. All I needed to do was show him some more money. Just a couple of thousand pound, that was all. I told him I wanted proof of Graham's 'crime' so that I could get a divorce. He couldn't resist. Saw the chance to make yet more from his dirty little scheme. Anyway, he got more than he expected, didn't he?"

"Did you kill him, Rose?"

"Of course I killed him. Evil little bastard, he was a waste of air."

"I think it's best now if we all go in the house and we'll get this sorted."

As he spoke Jordan reached towards her. She had dropped the hand holding the knife to her side and stood backlit by the light shining through the window. She was sobbing and shaking her head. Jordan moved closer towards her, calmly taking control.

There was a clatter from inside the house as Graham Matthews slid from the chair into a bloodied heap on the floor.

"Please, someone," he groaned, and reached a supplicating hand towards them.

Rosalind moved back onto the patio. It would be best for her to go inside, the boss had this sorted. Maybe there was something she could do for the man in the kitchen. She took a couple more steps. Another step and another. She was close to the other woman, but needed to move around her, to help the man possibly bleeding to death inside the house.

"Let me past, love. Let's just see if he's okay, yeah."

Time slowed as Rose Matthews lurched forward, raised her hand and reached out with the blade, slicing and slashing. Rosalind felt the fire in her belly, felt the warm gush of liquid and the world tipped for a moment.

"Leave him. Leave him," Rose screamed. "Leave us alone."

Rosalind heard Jordan's yell, she saw as he threw himself onto the woman, wrestling her to the ground, the knife skittering across the flags. She heard him telling her that she was under arrest for murder. That was odd because she wasn't dead. Or maybe she was, it was difficult to tell. Ah, maybe Graham was. Maybe it was that. It was hard to decide because everything was becoming faint and distant. She could hear the sirens, she could hear the boss yelling at her to stay awake, to stay with him. But really, she couldn't be bothered. She would just have a sleep. It had been a hard shift.

Chapter 66

DCI Richard Cross was smiling. It was a strange sight. It was such a rare occurrence that it made Jordan uneasy.

"So," he said as he leaned back in the chair and folded his hands over the swell of his belly, "three unlawful killings all wound up and tidy. That's going to look really good in our clear-up rates. Plus, I've got brownie points now with Waterloo and the City bods. Good stuff, DI Carr, yes very good stuff. You'll make sure everything is in order for the DPP. Don't want any last-minute hiccups."

"Yes, it's fine, sir. We've got a confession from Rose Matthews for the killing of Ben Harwood. We have the weapon and even the clothes she was wearing which have Ben Harwood's blood and DNA on them. She had tried to dispose of them in a bag of rubbish at the tip but fortunately they hadn't emptied the skips. There is video placing her at the scene and the hotel receptionist remembers seeing her. She tagged onto a group of other guests to gain access to the elevators, but we have some of that footage now. Once we stopped looking for Graham it all became clear. She has told us all she knows about the death of Beatrice Sharp, hearsay most of it but it's proving difficult to find all the details about her murder. Ben

Harwood did a good job of covering his tracks and with Graham Matthews dead there are always going to be a few unanswered questions.

"Time Tracers have been as helpful as they can but there's not much that we didn't already have. They are going out of business. The owner says he just can't continue, says he never imagined that what they were doing could be used for ill intent. In all honesty he lives in an insulated world and this has really shaken him. He's going back to teaching history, if he can find a job.

"We've released Beatrice's body and she'll go back to Newcastle to be buried with her mother. They'll have a joint funeral. I'd like to go up for that if it's possible, sir?"

Cross nodded.

"She left a will with instructions. It's as if she had an idea that what she was doing could possibly end badly. We'll never really know. The funeral directors are taking care of everything as there is no other next of kin. There was, as it happens, but Rose Matthews killed him."

"How is she?" Cross asked.

"Still in custody in hospital. She lost the baby, wrestling her to the ground couldn't have done any good but apparently the foetus probably wasn't viable anyway according to the tests they ran the day of the incident. Truly, sir, there wasn't any choice."

"No, the inspectorate has already decided that you acted in the only way possible under the circumstances. You mustn't blame yourself."

"It was a mess though, I know that. But even with the benefit of hindsight I don't know what we, what I, could have done differently."

"All the reports have exonerated you and the results speak for themselves. Cut yourself a bit of slack, DI Carr, it was complicated."

Jordan dredged up a smile, but he knew it would be a while before he came to terms with all that had happened.

"Sir. If there's nothing else, I wouldn't mind an early finish. If that's okay with you. I'm taking the wife out. She starts a new job on Monday and we haven't had a chance to celebrate yet. I have a couple of other things to do first."

"Yes. Off you go. Remember what I've said, Jordan, don't beat yourself up over things. You did the best you could."

As he walked back down the corridor Jordan couldn't help but smile. Yes, the boss had been kind and gracious, which was great, but it was because of the clear-up data and his own kudos as much as anything else. Fair enough, he had to take the flak when things went pear-shaped.

The loss of the baby made him terribly sad and he didn't know whether he would ever fully convince himself that he wasn't partly to blame.

* * *

The curtains were drawn over the windows of the side room. Jordan hung about trying to look inconspicuous until a nurse emerged pushing a trolley. She looked at him and then turned back.

"You've got a visitor. Are you okay with him coming in?"

"Yeah, that's fine." Rosalind Searle was sitting in a chair by the window. She was still hooked up to an infusion and her face was drawn and pale, but she looked better every time he came to see her.

"Hey, look at you, out of bed."

"I know. I'm fine, sir. They're talking about me going home next week."

"Brilliant. We need you back in work."

They both laughed. It would be a while before she was allowed back on duty. But she had already said that no stupid stomach wound was going to stop her.

"I've been authorised to tell you that you've been nominated for a bravery award. So, you might need your hair doing."

She laughed and raised a hand to her head.

"I'll get on to that, boss."

The door opened and they both turned to see Terry Denn peering into the room.

"Y'alright? Can I come in?"

"Yeah. Come on, wow this is nice. How are you, Terry?"

"I'm good, yeah."

Jordan looked at the DC and nodded.

"Go on, tell her."

"What– what's happened?"

"I'm back at work."

"Oh excellent." The two men laughed, and she looked back and forth between them, puzzled.

Terry sucked his teeth for a moment, shook his head.

"Okay, you'll hear it anyway. Some bright spark filmed me going arse over tit at the skatepark and put it online. It went viral."

Jordan laughed and Rosalind held onto her stomach as she began to giggle. "Ow, my stitches."

"The thing is," Jordan said, "there was a time stamp on the video and it was when Terry was supposed to be miles away beating up a lowlife mugger. Once the auntie was confronted with it, she withdrew her complaint. Said it was all a mistake."

"So, what did happen to him? I mean, someone beat him up."

"Dunno," Terry said. "Now then, what's this about an award, you jammy sod?"

Jordan looked across at Terry his eyebrows raised. The detective constable gave him what Nana Gloria would have termed 'an old-fashioned look'. It was obvious he wasn't going to be drawn on the issue and sometimes you just have to let things go.

List of characters

Detective Inspector Jordan Carr – Jamaican heritage. Married to Penny. They have one baby – Harry – whom he dotes on.

Elizabeth – Lizzie – Penny's sister.

Beatrice Sharp – Secretary at a printing company.

Vera Sharp – Beatrice's mother.

DCI Richard Cross – Late fifties. Impatient, overweight and short-tempered.

DCI Campbell – Waterloo senior officer.

Terry Denn – Mid twenties, newly promoted to plain clothes.

Sergeant Vivienne Bailey – SOCO team.

Detective Constable Rosalind Searle – Newly passed the detective exam.

Beverly Powell – Civilian collator.

Phyllis Grant (Phil) – Medical examiner.

Andy Grice – DCI from Liverpool Central.

Ben Harwood – Computer whizz who works at Time Tracers.

Jean Harwood – Ben's mother.

Graham Matthews – Financial advisor.

Rose Matthews – Married to Graham.

Stan Lipscowe – Owner of Time Tracers.

If you enjoyed this book, please let others know by leaving a quick review on Amazon. Also, if you spot anything untoward in the paperback, get in touch. We strive for the best quality and appreciate reader feedback.

editor@thebookfolks.com

www.thebookfolks.com

Also by Diane Dickson:

BODY BY THE DOCKS
BODY OUT OF PLACE

BURNING GREED
BRUTAL PURSUIT
BRAZEN ESCAPE
BRUTAL PURSUIT
BLURRED LINES

TWIST OF TRUTH
TANGLED TRUTH
BONE BABY
LEAVING GEORGE
WHO FOLLOWS
THE GRAVE
PICTURES OF YOU
LAYERS OF LIES
DEPTHS OF DECEPTION
YOU'RE DEAD
SINGLE TO EDINBURGH

Made in United States
North Haven, CT
27 October 2021

10640007R00152